Edward Henry Elwell

The Boys of Thirty-Five

A Story of a Seaport Town

Edward Henry Elwell

The Boys of Thirty-Five
A Story of a Seaport Town

ISBN/EAN: 9783744713450

Printed in Europe, USA, Canada, Australia, Japan

Cover: Foto ©Andreas Hilbeck / pixelio.de

More available books at **www.hansebooks.com**

THE

BOYS OF THIRTY-FIVE

A STORY OF A SEAPORT TOWN

BY

EDWARD HENRY ELWELL

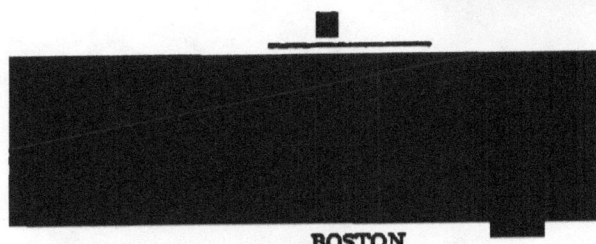

BOSTON
LEE AND SHEPARD, 47 FRANKLIN STREET
NEW YORK
CHAS. T. DILLINGHAM, 678 BROADWAY
1884

ALFRED MUDGE & SON, PRINTERS, BOSTON.

CONTENTS.

THE BOYS OF THIRTY-FIVE.

CHAPTER I.

THE SCENE OF ACTION.

I WAS born at Landsport, a town which boasted of
having the best harbor on the Atlantic coast. I am
particular to state this fact, because I have heard
that seven cities disputed for the honor of being the
birthplace of Homer, but I do not want any uncer-
tainty to hang about the place of my nativity. It
must be very annoying not to know where you were
born. I knew a young lady once who said she was
not born anywhere in particular; she was the daughter of a Methodist clergyman. I thought she always
had a bewildered look, as if she were trying to select
her birthplace out of the score of towns which
mingled confusedly in her memory. Another young
lady of my acquaintance was born on the Pacific
Ocean, on board an American ship, under the English flag, and was nursed by a Chinawoman. She
has always been troubled with perplexing doubts as
to her nationality, and then it is so awkward when

asked your birthplace to be compelled to say, "In about lat. 30° 15′ N., and lon. 140° 10′ E." Who would care to make a pilgrimage to such a birthplace?

I hasten, therefore, at the outset of my story, to give Landsport the credit of being the place where I was born. I have good authority for the statement, which I need not introduce here. Landsport is now a considerable city, but when I arrived there, on a dark day in December, at seven o'clock in the morning, it was but a bustling village, largely engaged in exporting lumber to the West Indies, in return for which its low-deck brigs brought home cargoes of molasses, great part of which was made into rum at its half-dozen distilleries. Some portion of the molasses, together with a good many "kintals" of salt fish, and a sufficient quantity of the rum to appease the thirst which the fish created, was exchanged for round hogs, cheese, butter, and lard, which the Vermonters, in their low red pungs, brought down through the Notch of the White Mountains. I took little note of these things, however, on my arrival, but devoted myself for a long time, as I have been informed, to sucking my thumb.

The first thing I can remember is my grandfather's house, in which I was born. I can see it now, in my mind's eye, although it was long since destroyed in the great fire which swept over the town, and was stayed just beyond the line on which the old house stood. It had seen many a troublous time, having been one of the few houses that escaped the flames when the British burned the town in 1775.

It stood close upon the sidewalk, and originally fronted the street; the town authorities declared that it encroached upon the roadway and proposed to set it back, but my grandfather threatened to shoot the first man who attempted to move it. I used to fancy him stalking up and down in front of the house, with his gun upon his shoulder.

His direful threat was not without its effect, for the old house remained undisturbed until after his death. He was a ship-master, and one dark night, while going down Long Wharf in Boston, he fell overboard and was drowned. All fear of the avenging gun being now removed, the selectmen turned the house about, presenting its gable end to the street. My grandmother weakly consented to this encroachment, but she always said that the town never kept its agreement to make the house as good as it was before She was only a widow, and kept no gun.

The old house was of but one story, but like a Dutch man-of-war, it had great breadth of beam, and was solidly built. The frame was of oak, and the corner posts stood out in the rooms with great prominence. I can see the "front room" now, with my grandmother sitting by the fire busily knitting. On the right as you entered was the buffet, a recess in the wall, extending half-way from the ceiling to the floor, and forming a sort of cupboard, with a curtain in front.   Here my grandmother kept her best "chany" set; but the chief ornament of the buffet was a great naval pitcher, with a picture on it of two frigates engaged in battle, and guns and flags crossed in the foreground.   Inscribed upon it was the sentiment, "Success to our Infant Navy."   I used to wonder who was the infant Navy, not doubting that he was somebody's baby.   My grandmother, whose father had sailed with Commodore Truxtun, said the picture commemorated Truxtun's victory over the French frigate *La Vengeance*, away back in 1800, but this information did not much enlighten me.

I had good reason to remember that pitcher, for it owed its destruction to one of my youthful indiscretions.   One day, with many injunctions to carry it carefully, I was sent with it to the house of a neighbor who had wished to borrow it.   The neighbor lived at some little distance, and as I went on my way, with my precious burden, it occurred to me that it would be interesting to ascertain how fast I could walk with my eyes shut.   I tried the experiment, and thought I was going on in a remarkably straight line, when my progress was suddenly arrested by a violent shock and a great crash.   I opened my eyes, and was much surprised to find that I had run into a stone post that stood on the edge of the sidewalk, and that the great naval pitcher lay in fragments at my feet.

My heart sank within me, for I knew my grand-mother set great store by that pitcher.   As I looked sorrowfully down at the fragments I saw that the picture of the ships engaged in combat was unbroken. I took heart at this, for I knew that it was in one of those ships that my great-grandfather had fought, and that my grandmother took great pride in that picture.   Picking up the fragment I ran home, and bursting into the house exclaimed, "I saved the ships, grandma'am!"

"Saved the ships, child; why, what have you done with my pitcher?"

"It hit against a post and broke all to pieces, but I saved the ships," said I, with an air worthy of the descendant of a naval hero.

"What a pity!   But did n't you hurt you, child?"

That was all she said.   If I had been a boy of to-day I should have inwardly remarked, "Is n't she a bully grandmother?"   But being forty years behind the times, I only said, "No, ma'am," and ran off to my play.

Next beyond the buffet was the fireplace.   I re-member the brass-headed andirons that stood in it, because there was a small hole in the top of one of them into which I used to drop all the pins I could find, for the pleasure of unscrewing the top and taking them out.

We used to sit by the hearth on the winter evenings and listen to the stories my grandmother told of the time when my grandfather brought her home to the old house, from Salem, where he married her. Mother used to say that grandmother was the Salem beauty in her day, but grandmother never said so. I know she was a comely old lady. She wore a calash, and somehow I always think of her now as having a sort of old-fashioned chaise-top over her head.

She used to tell us that when she came home to my great-grandfather's house he owned one or two negro slaves, and that when they misbehaved my great-grandmother had them tied up to the apple-trees in the garden and flogged. I used to picture her a very stern old lady, with a big whip in her hand.

One stormy winter night, as we sat by the blazing wood fire, on the big wooden settees, the high backs of which kept off the draughts from the rattling windows, she told us of the great storm when so many vessels were lost on the coast. A furious gale raged all night, and the snow piled in high drifts almost to the tops of the low windows. Such snow-storms as they used to have in the old times! There is nothing like them in these degenerate days.

My grandmother said that my uncle Benjamin, who was a printer, was obliged to rise very early on the morning following the storm, and groping in the fireplace for a coal with which to light his candle (there were no friction matches in those days), his hand fell upon a human face! He was much startled, but presently, succeeding in lighting his candle, he saw a man lying at full length upon the hearth. It required some effort to arouse him, but when at last he was able to sit up and speak he told this story: He was a poor fisherman whose craft had been dashed against the wharf until she sank, he barely escaping with his life. At midnight, in the driving storm, he struggled through the snow-drifts up into the town, trying every door, but finding all fastened until he came to my grandfather's. Here he entered and sought to warm himself by the dying em'ers, until he fell asleep.

Doors were often left unfastened all night in those primitive days. In my boyhood a stout bar at the top was all the fastening of the door.

After these stories my grandmother would rake the ashes over the embers to preserve some coals for the morning fire, and I would be sent to bed in one of the great chambers of the garret. (There were no "attics" then.) There I would lie and listen to the wind whistling in the great chimney which ran up through the centre of the house.

One of those garret chambers was my play-ground on winter days when the snow was too deep to admit of my going out of doors. Heavy oaken beams ran along the gable end of the garret, just above the floor, and on these I used to marshal my company of toy soldiers, and fire my tiny cannon. I had, however, more of a nautical than a military turn of mind, and used to "make believe" the garret was a ship in which I made long voyages. Great beams ran across near the ridge-pole, and one of these I could reach by means of the flight of steps that led up to the scuttle in the roof. Fastening a rope in a loop, from one end of the beam to the other, to serve as a foot-rope, I regarded the beam as a yard on the mast of the ship, while the ladder by which it was reached was the ratlines.

Once, when out on this yard-arm, taking in sail in a tremendous gale of wind, the foot-rope swung out from under my feet, doubtless owing to a sudden lurch of the ship; and turning a summersault I fell head-foremost into a barrel of feathers. Nothing was seen of me for a time but a very lively pair of heels, and I might have smothered in the feathers if

Si Sumner, the ship's mate, had not cried, " Shiver my timbers!" and rushed to the rescue. Si had great command of the nautical vocabulary, and I rated him as a first-class seaman.

When dragged out by the heels I had very little breath in me, but the feathers had broken my fall, and I was not seriously hurt. In my struggles to release myself I had grasped a handful of feathers, and when I opened my hand something fell from it on to the floor. Si picked it up and declared that it was a piece of gold money. I told my mother that I saw it on the bottom of the ocean, and dived over-board after it, but grandmother, while trying to brush the feathers from my clothes with a damp brush, said she knew better.

The feathers had been emptied from an old bed for the purpose of cleansing, and doubtless the coin had been brought home by one of my sea-faring uncles, and had accidentally found its way into the bed. It was customary in those days to conceal money between the beds. I have kept the coin all these years as a memento of my early sea-faring days, and not long since, in turning over some old keepsakes, I came upon it. It is as bright and fresh as when coined, although it bears date of 1730. It is a Por-tuguese coin, of the reign of John V., and bears the inscription, "*In hoc signo vinces.*" In that sign I conquered, for the finding of the coin diverted attention from my perilous adventure, and I was permitted to continue my voyage without further reproof.than an admonition against going on to the yard-arm in a gale of wind.

There was a large garden in the rear of my grandfather's house, and the day had been when it was still larger. It once ran through to Fore Street, but my grandfather had sold off several lots, and in my boyhood it was bounded at the foot by Chaddock's orchard. The old wide-spreading apple-trees in Chaddock's dropped their ripe fruit in the tall grass, from which the red and yellow apples peeped out temptingly. From the top of the fence I used to gaze upon them much as the ancient Israelites looked upon the Promised Land. But away through the vista of the trees there was a glimpse of a back door, seldom open, but always looking as if some grim personage was ready to issue from it and pounce upon any trespasser. Undoubtedly there were raids made upon those apples in my time, but I never knew a boy to go beyond the fence and tell of it.

In my grandfather's garden there were two very large apple-trees, the Pearmain and the Bitter-sweet. The Pearmain was a wide-spreading tree, branching near the ground, into which I could climb and nestle among the embowered boughs. I was in this tree when Bill Truman fell from it, and, striking on his head, lay insensible on the ground until his father came and carried him into the house. I remember how I stole away with a deep awe upon me, thinking poor Bill was dead. But he was a hard-headed boy, and lived many a long year after.

The Bitter-sweet, unlike the Pearmain, had a tail, straight stem, which I could never climb, but by way of compensation it had a large cavity near the ground, which served me for a cavern, in which many precious possessions were hidden.

On one side of the garden there rose the high dead wall of the stage-coach company's stable, broken only in the basement by a long row of square apertures admitting light to the stalls, and out of which the horses used to poke their noses for a whiff of fresh air. I used to make acquaintance with them as I played in the garden, and fancied they got to know me. One, whose mild eyes I always recognized, often greeted me with a gentle whinny, which I interpreted to mean " good morning." I have since thought it was only a reminder of the apple he was accustomed to receive at my hands.

I remember one long sunny afternoon, during which I was all alone, at the foot of the garden, engaged in the tantalizing pursuit of a butterfly. The gayly painted creature seemed to enter into the sport with

me, hovering about my head, and then, as I threw up
my cap at it, mounting higher, as if in mockery of my
vain attempts to catch it. It led me a long chase
among the flowers, still hovering about, until something of its own light-heartedness took possession of
me, and I rejoiced in its companionship, the long,
bright hours gliding away like a pleasant dream.   I
sometimes wonder if I have ever been as happy
in the pursuit of the world's allurements as I was
when chasing the butterfly in my grandfather's garden.

On the side of the garden opposite the stable there
was a vacant lot used as a lumber-yard, beyond which
ran the long building of the twine factory, with many
small windows.   At the head of the lumber-yard,
fronting the street, stood a building occupied by Si
Sumner's father as a joiner shop.   In the second
story of this building, approached by an outside
flight of stairs in the rear, was a long-disused school-
room in which one of the old " masters " had taught.

We boys used to climb the long flight of stairs,
which made a sharp turn above the first story, and
from the upper landing peer in at the windows.
Once we got possession of the key, and entering, ran
riot over the deserted benches. On one of these
were the initials " J. C.," cut large with a grand flour-
ish around them. The owner of those initials after-

wards cut a great figure in the world's school-room, and his name stands graven there still.

Do you see, as I do, the low, unpainted cottage, with its gable end close upon the sidewalk, the great stable standing back from the street on one side of it, the old school-house on the other, and the long garden stretching away behind it? It is all in my mind's eye only, for now the ground "where once the garden smiled" is covered with great blocks of brick and stone, and Chaddock's apple-trees have given place to store-houses and workshops.

Having set the stage, let me now introduce the characters who are to act upon it.

CHAPTER II.

IN WHICH THE READER MAKES SOME NEW ACQUAINT-
ANCES, AND A GREAT BATTLE IS FOUGHT.

ONE morning in spring, when the weather had grown warm enough to enable us to play on the sunny side of the street, a half-dozen boys were engaged in a game of rolly-pooly on the sidewalk in front of the house in which Si Sumner lived, which stood opposite my grandfather's.   In the game of rolly-pooly a ball was rolled into a slight depression in the ground.   Ed Thompson had the ball, and he tossed it into the air just as a gentleman was passing, with a small boy at his side.   The gentleman caught the ball as it came down, and critically examined it.   It was not a cast-iron ball, such as is now used in the noble game of base-ball, but was stuffed with woollen yarn and india-rubber, and covered with soft leather.   Ed Thompson's mother had made it for him, and we considered it a great success, Si Sumner's sister having signally failed in an attempt to a similar manufacture.   She produced a cylinder instead of a globe, and when Ben Hunter caught sight of it he cried out, —

"Hallo, Si, where did you get that pepper-box?"

"Si's pepper-box" it remained to the end.

The gentleman seemed satisfied with his examination of the ball, and turning to Ed Thompson handed him a fourpence 'alfpenny, gave the ball to the boy by his side, and passed on.

Ed Thompson, who was a shy little fellow, stood dumbfounded, while Ben Hunter cried out, —

"That's John Neal, confound his impudence!"

Ben was a big, bullying boy, with a tongue of his own, and was never backward in the expression of his opinions.

"What shall we do now?" said Joe Jameson, whose turn it was to roll; "he's carried off the ball!"

At that moment Ben Hunter cried, —

"Here comes 'Hurrah for Jackson!'"

Looking up street we· saw a gentleman driving down in a chaise. He was a big, round, jolly-looking man, and as he passed we all gathered on the edge of the sidewalk and shouted, "Hurrah for Jackson!" whereupon the gentleman in the chaise lifted his hat and bowed and smiled.

This was the Hon. Albert Smith, who, Ben said, was a member of Congress and a great admirer of Gen. Jackson. I afterwards heard him make a political speech, in which, in true *ad captandum* style, he charged the Whigs with putting a tax on molasses, "an article," said he, "I am very fond of!"

" I tell you what," said Ben, after the Hon. Albert
had passed, " let's go into the stable and play the
battle of New Orleans; Gen. Jackson, you know,
whipped the Britishers there."

"Agreed," cried we all, and into the stable we
went. Now this stable of the stage-coach company
was a famous play-ground for us boys. As I have
said, it stood back from the street, and there had
once been great gates in front of it. These were
now gone, but the high gate-posts and broken wall
on each side remained, and I used to fancy them the
entrance to a ruined castle. The ground on which
the stable stood fell off in the rear, and the basement was occupied by the stage horses, while the
first floor, on a level with the street, was filled with
stage-coaches and sleigh-coaches, in which on rainy
days we sat and told stories, or played hide-and-seek.
Many a journey we took in those old coaches as they
stood in the gloomy recesses of the carriage-room.
It was a scene of great interest for us when one of
them was drawn out and the horses put to, and the
driver pulled on his big gloves and mounted the box,
and the coach went rolling out of the gateway.

On one side of the door, as you entered the carriage-room, stood an immense grain-chest, the contents of which were conducted by a spout to the
stable below.

"This," said Ben, "is the fort, and those bags of oats leaning against the well beyond are the cotton bales with which Gen. Jackson defended the city. I am Gen. Jackson, and Joe Jameson must be Gen. Packenham, the commander of the Britishers. Choose your men."

"I'm not going to be a Britisher to be beaten by you," said Joe.

But the boys all declared he was just the fellow to lead the invading forces, Si Sumner sagaciously remarking that you could not tell who would be whipped until after the battle was fought.

Thus flattered and entreated, Joe was compelled to take command of the British army, and the commanders selected their forces, each choosing a boy in turn. I fell into the ranks of the British, and was made second in command.

Gen. Jackson, with his forces, immediately took possession of the fort by mounting the grain-chest, when Jim Norton, who was on our side, cried out, —

"What shall we use for weapons?"

"There's a pile of empty meal-bags," said Gen. Jackson, ever ready in resources; "let's take them."

Every man armed himself with a meal-bag, and then Gen. Packenham called a council of war, to determine on the best plan of attack. I was for undermining and blowing up the enemy's fort, but the general decided on carrying his works by storm.

Meantime Gen. Jackson had been busily engaged in fortifying his position by placing a line of cotton bales (bags filled with oats) along the edge of the grain-chest. Seeing this, our commander decided on dividing his forces, and while one division, under his own command, made an assault in front, I was to lead a brigade over the tops of the bags of oats still standing against the wall on one side of the fort.

With a loud shout the assaulting party rushed on, while I led my forces silently over the grain-bags, intending to surprise the enemy. But Gen. Jackson had his eyes about him, and immediately detached a portion of his forces, under command of Si Sumner, to beat us off, while he led the defence in front.

Loud were the shouts and dire the conflict when the contending forces met. Thick flew the dust of the battle as the meal-bags waved in air and fell with many a whack on the heads and shoulders of the assailants, who, being compelled to fight from a much lower level, were at a disadvantage. They, however, contrived to give the defenders of the fort many a wipe in the face, which never failed to leave a mealy impression.

Meantime my attempt at a surprise had ended disastrously. The grain-bags afforded but an insecure

footing, and Gen. Sumner met our advance so gallantly that, together with one half my forces (in the
person of Jim Norton), I was thrown to the ground.

At this critical moment there rushed on to the
field of battle a boy with a flaming red head and a
broad grin on his face, who shouted, —

"Go it, boys, I 'm with ye!"

This was Tim Bunce, whose perpetual grimaces
and comical antics marked him as the clown of the
neighborhood.   No sooner did Gen. Packenham
catch sight of him than he exclaimed, —

"A re-enforcement, boys! Come on, Tim!"

Nothing loath, Tim grinned and bobbed his head,
and scraped his splay foot, shouting, "I'm going
right in among 'em!" With this he made a dash at
the fort, and in attempting to climb the wall,
grabbed one of the bags of oats and brought it down
upon his own head. The string broke, and out
poured the oats, nearly smothering Tim.

But Gen. Packenham shouted, "A breach, a
breach! Now, by St. George, the day is ours." And
heading a column, made a dash for the wall. The
defenders filled the breach, and met our advance in
the most gallant manner. Meal-bags were now discarded, and fists came into play. Blows rained thick
and fast on our defenceless heads, but we struck
back stoutly, and Tim Bunce, rising, with his great

shock of red hair filled with oats, grasped Si Sumner by the leg, and brought him down into a sitting posture with a terrible thump. Before Si could regain his breath, Jim Norton seized his other leg, and the two brought Si down upon the ground with a lamentable rent in his nether garment, which had caught on a nail in the lid of the grain-chest.

"A prisoner! A wounded prisoner!" we shouted, as poor Si, with a very crestfallen air, was led off and placed in one of the coaches under guard.

At this moment there appeared on the scene a tall, slim boy, who stood at the entrance of the carriage-room, with an expression of mild wonder on his face and a huge bag on his back. Gen. Jackson, catching sight of him, shouted, —

"A re-enforcement for our side! We want you, Hay-bag!" and reaching down from the wall seized the astonished youth by the collar, and, spite of his struggles and remonstrances, dragged him into the fort, bag and all.

The new-comer was "Hay-bag" Ross, whose father drove one of those long, narrow truck teams that used to block up the whole width of the street when turned across it to take on a load. His sleepy old horse was accustomed to stand and doze in the shafts, which were supported by a pole which hung from one of them, during the long summer afternoons, in front of the furrier's at the corner of the street. To provide provender for the beast, Hay-bag was sent by his father with a bag to gather up the wisps of hay left by the teamsters after feeding their cattle on the wharves, and thus gained the nickname by which he was known among the boys. On this occasion he was returning from one of these forays with a bag well filled. Gen. Jackson seized upon the bag to fill the breach in his wall, while Hay-bag stood looking on, the picture of despair.

The bag of hay was not so solid a defence as the bag of oats had been, and Tim Bunce soon whisked it around and was about pulling it off the wall when the other end was seized by the defenders of the fort. In the struggle, the hay fell out, and Gen. Jackson, seizing great armfuls of it, showered it down upon our heads and upturned faces. Half smothered by this novel ammunition, we withdrew to concert a new plan of attack.

Gen. Packenham declared that the wall must be scaled, and seizing the long cross-bar that secured the great doors of the stable, he placed one end of it on the ground and detailed Tim Bunce to hold the other end against the top of the wall while he led a forlorn hope up this scaling ladder into "the imminent deadly breach." He had already advanced half-way up the bar when Gen. Jackson gave the end resting on the top of the wall a vigorous kick, and down it went, our commander falling across it with a violence that knocked the wind out of him.

"Are ·you hurt, Joe?" said Gen. Jackson, looking down from the wall.

" Pretty bad," groaned Joe.

"Well, never mind, you 've got to die, any way. Gen. Packenham was killed, you know."

" I 'll be hanged if I 'll die," retorted Joe, but he had no stomach for further fight.

Our general being thus disabled, the leadership devolved upon me, as second in command. Casting about for a new method of attack, my eyes fell upon the pole of a stage-coach standing in the back part of the carriage-room, in a direct line with the fort. A new idea flashed upon me. Calling Jim Norton into conference with me, I proposed using the stage-coach as a battering-ram. Jim was a little dubious about it, but I told him I had read about battering-rams in my history book; that in old times they always used them when besieging a city, and that it was sure to frighten the enemy out of their wits, or — what would be still better — out of the fort.

Much impressed with my superior military education, Jim fell into the plan. and we proceeded at once to put it into execution.

The enemy were busily engaged in strengthening

their walls with more bags of oats, and did not at first observe our operations. Detailing Tim Bunce to manage the pole, I set the rest of my forces to pushing the coach down upon the fort, while I mounted the box to direct operations.

The coach was heavy, and it required the united strength of my entire army to start it, but once in motion it acquired momentum as it rolled on. Tim tugged at the pole, dancing and capering about it, declaring that he was "a whole team and a horse to let," while I, standing on the box, in all the majesty of conscious victory, shouted, —

"Surrender, you villains, or I'll knock your walls about your ears!"

Startled by the formidable engine coming down upon them, the enemy began to scramble out of the fort, but Gen. Jackson restrained his men with a strong arm, and laughed us to scorn.

"Come on with your one-horse team," he shouted.

My purpose had been to have the pole strike the bags on the wall of the fort, and thus make a breach, through which we were to rush in while the enemy were in a demoralized condition. But Tim could not elevate the pole sufficiently to strike the bags, and the result was that it went crashing into the side of the grain-chest, staving a great hole in it.

The shock threw the garrison off their feet, some

tumbling down to the ground, while I was knocked
flat on to the top of the coach.

Before I could regain my feet I heard a gruff voice
exclaiming, "What does all this mean?" and looking
over the side of the coach I saw the burly figure of
Joe Jameson's father, who had charge of the stable,
entering the door with a whip in his hand. At that
moment Gen. Jackson was descending from the walls
of his demolished fort; and as he had the reputation
of being the leader in all mischief going on, Mr.
Jameson seized him by the collar and began to ply
his whip vigorously about Ben's legs. Ben danced
and shouted, "It was n't me, Mr. Jameson, it was
Harry Ingersoll," meaning me.

I thought it was now time to beat a retreat; particularly as my army, deeming discretion the better
part of valor, had already retired in disorder, some
hiding in the coaches in the dark corners, while
others scuttled out of the door. Crawling down over
the rear of the coach, I dodged behind another car-
riage, and made my way out of a back door that
overlooked the manure heap. Scrambling over this,
I jumped down into my grandfather's garden.

I was proceeding up the garden, congratulating myself that I had retired in good order, when I heard a
voice crying, —

" Help a feller down, won't ye, Harry?"

Looking up, I espied Tim Bunce hanging by the seat of his trousers near the top of a stack of bean-poles. The poles had been placed on end, leaning against the stable wall, their tops nearly reaching to a small door that opened out of the carriage-room, which on this side of the stable was high above the ground. Tim in his hasty retreat had jumped out of this door on to the tops of the poles, and in trying to make his way down them had been caught in the rear by a sharp spur on one of the poles.

"Why, Tim," said I, "what are you doing up there?"

"Hanging up to dry," he replied, with a grimace; "but say, can't ye help a feller down?"

"Hush! you 'll call Mr. Jameson to that door, with his whip."

Poor Tim cast one eye up at the door and the other to the ground below, and gave another wriggle, but all in vain.

"I can't reach you, Tim, but I'll call grandmother."

"Don't call your grandmarm," replied Tim, with an agonized grin; "I s'pose I'm all tore out behind!"

Just then, sure enough, Mr. Jameson appeared at the door above. "Oh, ho!" said he, "you are there, are you? Just hang on, Tim, till I call round for you!"

The prospect of such a call was more than Tim could endure. He writhed and struggled, something gave way, and down he came on all fours.

"Are you hurt, Tim?" I asked, with some concern, spite of the comical appearance he cut.

"No, but I 'spect I shall be if I stop here." And with that he scuttled away out of the garden.

CHAPTER III.

I ENTER THE GRAMMAR SCHOOL FOR BOYS.

IT was with quaking hearts that six of us boys one morning approached the door of Master Gorham's grammar school. We had purposely absented ourselves from the annual examination, but had now been sent by Miss Cummings, the teacher of the primary school, to pass a supplementary examination; so we had gained nothing by staying away, but, on the contrary, had a more terrible ordeal to pass than if we had attended the examination at the proper time. I have learned since that nothing is ever gained by shirking a trial or a task, and that those get on best who meet every duty promptly.

We approached the school-house at a snail's pace, with fear and trembling. It was a long, low brick building of one story, with a double row of posts in front, set so that it was necessary to twist and turn in order to pass between them. I never knew why they were thus placed, unless it was to symbolize the difficulty of getting into the grammar school, or to encourage the boys in the practice of gymnastic exercises. The usual custom of the boys when rushing out of school was to place each hand on a post and leap over the outside row. We, however, were content to worm our way in between them, and would have been glad, on the whole, if we had stuck fast among them.

As we entered the vestibule that ran across the whole width of the building, we saw a placard hanging under a small window that looked in upon the master's desk, with the word " Late " upon it. After this placard was hung out no tardy scholar could find admittance. We were tardy enough, but we knew the sign was not for us and so knocked timidly at the door.

A monitor gave us admission, and we found ourselves in the dread presence of the master and one hundred and fifty school-boys, all peeping furtively at us from behind their books. We were presently ranged in a row in the aisle, and the master heard each read a passage in " Worcester's Third Book "; then each was given a sum in arithmetic to solve, after which we were assigned to seats on the lower benches nearest the master's desk. The more advanced scholars, according to their rank, sat farther back on the higher benches, the floor inclining towards the doors, which were placed on each side of the master's desk. The benches, without backs, but with desks in front of them, ran across the width of the school-room, leaving space at each end for an aisle and also for a line of single desks placed at intervals against the walls.

These single desks were occupied by the monitors, for the school was conducted on the Lancastrian plan, then in great vogue as an economic and effective method of enabling one master to teach any number of scholars,— from one hundred to a thousand. This mutual or monitorial plan was thought to be an admirable method of converting pupils into teachers. The more advanced scholars taught those less advanced, and so saved the expense of assistant teachers. There was great enthusiasm about this system, both in England and in this country, and its introduction by Joseph Lancaster gave an impetus to popular education in both countries. It did not produce the highest results, but it led to the adoption of a better system.

In Master Gorham's school the Lancastrian plan was principally applied to the reading exercises. The whole school was divided in "drafts," distributed among the monitors occupying the side desks and the head monitor's desk at the rear end of the room. All the drafts were heard at the same time, and as one boy was reading aloud in each simultaneously with a boy in all the others, — some twenty or thirty in number, — there was a rare hubbub during the reading exercise. A passer-by might have thought bedlam had broken loose.

Yet the general confusion of tongues did not disturb the exercises of each draft. The boys stood around the desk of the monitor, in a semicircle, extending from the wall of the school-house on one side of the desk to the other side, and being thus shut in among themselves, paid no attention to what was going on in the other drafts.

For the preservation of order a special monitor was appointed whose duty it was to walk around the aisles during the reading exercise, and to whom the reading monitors reported any act of insubordination or infringement of rules. On the raised platform on which stood the master's desk there were two lower desks, one on each side of his, occupied by four monitors, whose duty it was to keep an oversight of the school, and call out any boy who might be detected in mischief or neglecting his studies.

A certain number of benches were also given in charge of a monitor during the exercise in penmanship. While this was going on the master sat on his high stool at his desk making and mending quill pens. When a scholar grew tired of writing, or thought his pen needed mending, he held up his hand and the monitor came and mended his pen or corrected his position in holding it.

On the memorable day of my entrance into this temple of learning, Jim Norton and I were assigned seats together on one of the long benches. The boy whose seat was next to mine welcomed me with a hideous grimace, which I resented with a scowl. Presently I saw him dexterously twitch a hair from the head of the boy on the other side of him. The boy thus assaulted seemed accustomed to these little eccentricities of his seat-mate, for he merely rubbed his scalp and shrank farther away from his tormentor. Not long after, while my attention was turned in another direction, I felt a sharp twinge, and turning my head quickly I became aware that my ingenious companion had employed the hair so feloniously obtained in sawing my ear. I immediately seized his ear and gave it a twist that caused him to howl with pain. In an instant I was started by the cry of, —

"Ingersoll!"

The monitor had witnessed our little by-play, and I was called out to await condign punishment. How my heart sank within me as I saw the master approaching and glaring at me over his spectacles! He was a short, thick-set man, irreverently nick-named "Duck-Legs" by the boys.

"Hold out your hand," said he.

I advanced a timid palm, but immediately

snatched it away again as the ferule was about to descend upon it, getting only a rap upon the knuckles.

"Go to your seat, sir, and don't let me hear from you again." Glad of any dismissal, I crept back to my seat, to be greeted with a diabolical leer by my friend of the hair. I began to hate that boy, and as I passed behind him to my seat I gave his hair a twitch which caused him to give his immediate attention to his book.

When the hour of recess arrived we tumbled out into the school-yard in a tumultuous crowd. Feeling a little lonesome among so many strange boys, Si Sumner, Jim Norton, and I got together in a corner to compare notes.

"What's the name of that fellow who sits next me?" I inquired.

"That's Bully Hawkins," replied Si; "he's the worst boy in school."

"Well, he won't bully me," was my reply.

At this moment Ben Hunter, who had entered the school at the previous term, and felt himself quite at home in it, approached and cried out, —

"Look here, Harry, Bully Hawkins is after you. He says he's bound to give you a thrashing, but don't you be afraid of him."

"Who's afraid?" I replied, with an assumption

of courage I by no means felt. I determined not to seek a quarrel with Hawkins, but not to submit to any bullying by him.

The yard was by this time all alive with boys racing across it, and seeing Joe Jameson among them, I ran to join him. On my way I happened to pass by Bully Hawkins, who put out his foot and tripped me up, so that I fell headlong to the ground. Rising again, not much hurt, but wild with rage, I dashed at my tormentor, who stood at a little distance with an insolent grin upon his ugly mug. He was startled by my sudden onset, but stood his ground and returned blow for blow.

"A ring! a ring!" shouted the boys who saw this sudden engagement, while Ben Hunter cried out, —

"Fair play, boys. Give it to him, Harry!"

My blood was up, and Hawkins was hardly prepared for so impetuous an assault. He was a stout fellow, but wasn't so mad as I was, and besides, had the consciousness of being in the wrong I went into close quarters with him, in a rough-and-tumble fight, and his superior strength was beginning to tell against me, when I hit him a blow on the nose that set it bleeding, and caused him to yell with pain. I followed this up with blows about his head and ears, when he cried "Enough!" and slunk out of the ring.

The boys, many of whom had been the victims of his tyranny, set up a shout, and my friends clustered around me and congratulated me on my victory. I was the hero of the hour, while poor Bully was wiping his nose in a corner. One small boy said, —

"That pays him for pinching me."

Another shouted, —

"Hurrah for Harry; he's whipped Bully Hawkins!"

All except a small cluster of his cronies were ready to rejoice over Hawkins's defeat. He seemed to feel this more than the flogging he had got, and casting a contemptuous and defiant glance at the exulting crowd, he came forward, with his handkerchief at his nose, and said to me, —

"Ingersoll, you fight like a tiger, but I guess you gave me about what I deserved. I'm willing to be friends if you are."

These frank words caused an immediate revulsion of my feelings towards him, and grasping his hand I exclaime —

"All right, Hawkins; I hope you are not much hurt."

The boys set up a shout at this scene of reconciliation, and as the bell rang at this moment we all went tumbling into school again.

There was a monitor of the school-yard, whose duty

it was at recess time to set down, slate in hand, the names of those boys who made a disturbance or were loud and boisterous in their play, to be reported to the master.

Charlie Gardiner was monitor on this occasion, but he took care to keep out of the way and see nothing of the fight between Hawkins and myself.

"Gardiner," said Master Gorham, "there was a great noise during recess, and I must punish you for making no report of it."

Thereupon Charlie was feruled for the first and last time in his life, while Hawkins and I, who had been the guilty cause of all the disturbance, escaped scot free. Thus impartially is justice administered in this world.

After this introduction I got on well with the boys, and soon began to take an interest in my studies. It was not all fun at Master Gorham's school. He was a strict disciplinarian, and when seated at his high desk, with his monitors on either side of him, he was like a general on the battle-field, keeping his forces well in hand. Then the school was on its good behavior, and every boy was busy with his books. Somehow a gleam of the master's eye made us all very diligent, and we took rapid strides up the hill of knowledge, — for a time. There were, however, moments of relaxation. Of an afternoon it was the master's wont to thrust his broken cowhide, doubled up like a whip with its lash, into his pocket, both ends sticking out, and waddle up the school-room to the upper benches, where he gave his attention to the more advanced scholars.

We boys on the lower benches, though still under the eyes of the vigilant monitors, were then left pretty much to our own devices. How lazily the hours dragged along on those sunny afternoons, as we loitered over our books, with an occasional diversion into other studies than those laid down for our pursuit!

It was on one of those drowsy afternoons that I heard a half-suppressed giggle ripple over the benches behind me, and turning my head, caught sight for an instant of a spectacle that nearly sent me off into a loud guffaw. In the upper left-hand corner of the school-room there was a small closet partitioned off with boards. The tradition in the school was that this was a prison pen for the confinement of truants and other incorrigible offenders, but I never knew it to be put to such a use. We smaller boys stood in some awe of it, and had never ventured to peep into it. High up on that side of the closet, looking down the school-room, was a small round hole in the wall, presumably made for the admission of air and light. What I saw on turning my head was a comical, grimacing face at this hole, surmounted by a tuft of fiery red hair, which seemed to leave a streak of light behind it as the face quickly vanished.

All the boys on the benches in my neighborhood were instantly on the alert to catch another glimpse of this comical visitant. Presently the face again appeared, with a more diabolical grimace than before, and the titter among the boys became louder than at first; it attracted the attention of the monitors, who looked around in vain for the cause of it. We boys at once bent studiously over our books, still, however, casting a furtive glance over our shoulders in the direction of the closet. Once more the mysterious visage appeared, and being observed this time by a larger number of the scholars than at first, an irrepressible laugh went up.

Master Gorham was at once aroused and instantly demanded the cause of the disturbance. As he was at the upper end of the school-room, beyond the line of the closet, he could not see the orifice in its wall, and the monitors, not having observed the face, could not account for the merriment among the boys, nor could they call out a whole bench at once. The matter grew more mysterious every moment, and there was a threatening aspect in the master's face as he strode down the school-room to investigate the cause of this untimely merriment.

All eyes were now directed towards the orifice in the closet wall. Presently the face appeared again, this time directing contemptuous grimaces towards the master, whose back was turned towards it as he hurried down the aisle. The boys were now nearly beyond control. Some rose in their seats; others laughed aloud. The master, turning quickly around, caught a glimpse of the visage as it disappeared from the hole. At that moment, just as a feeling of awe was creeping over the boys, and silence reigned, a tremendous crash was heard. The master rushed to the closet door, tore it open, and instantly dragged out by the collar the shrinking figure of Tim Bunce.

The boys were now all on their feet. "Sit down!" shouted the master as he dragged Tim down the aisle and set him on his feet in front of the desk. We dropped into our seats, but kept our eyes fastened on the scene in front of us.

"How came you in that closet, sir?" said the master, who by this time had drawn his cowhide from his pocket.

"I — I went in," replied Tim, very humbly, at the same time casting a squint at the boys from the corner of his eye that nearly upset our gravity again.

"And what did you go in for, sir?"

"Ju-just to see how it would seem."

"Well, sir, you'll now learn how it seems to get a

cowhiding." And with that the lash came down on Tim's back, and he began to caper about in a way that made it difficult for the master to control him, but he got a terrible thrashing and was sent howling to his seat.

It appeared that he had stolen into the closet before-the arrival of the master, and finding there a broken bench, had placed it against the wall and climbed upon it. When once he looked out of the hole it was not in Tim's nature to resist making faces, and the rest followed as a matter of course. The crash heard was occasioned by the bench slipping out from under him and throwing him down upon the floor.

Poor Tim! he was the occasion of a good deal of fun, much of which was involuntary on his part. He was not a brilliant scholar, and stumbled sadly in his reading. I remember on one occasion we were reading in the draft of James Moore, the head monitor, when the lesson was in "Worcester's Fourth Book," being Goldsmith's account of the golden eagle. Of this proud bird it was said, "How hungry soever he may be, he never stoops to carrion." It fell to Tim to read this paragraph, which he rendered thus, "How — hungry — soever he may be — he never *stops to carry on*."

"He would be a fool to stop to carry on while he was hungry," said Moore, whereat we all laughed.

But Tim was not the author of all the mischief going on, however fertile he might be in blunders. 'What do you think, boys," said little Ed Thompson, one day, "there's been a row over on Cotton Street, and Ben Hunter was n't in it!" This was almost incredible, for every piece of mischief was charged upon Ben, and he seldom took the trouble to deny it. Ben had a cool assurance, an amount of "check," as we should now say, that carried him through everything.

There was a cellar under the school-house, in which was stored the wood burned in the box stoves for the heating of the school-room in the winter term. It was the custom of the master to appoint two boys, in turn, to build the fires of a morning. One day, when Ben Hunter and Joe Jameson had performed that task, Joe said to me, with a mysterious wink, —

"You 'll see some fun to-day."

"What 's up?" I inquired.

"Never you mind, you 'll hear something that 'll astonish old Duck-Legs."

As the school-bell rang at that moment I was forced to be content with this mysterious intimation of some impending event of a startling character. The forenoon passed away, and nothing remarkable happened. I noticed, however, at recess, that Joe and Ben held a whispered conference and parted with the injunction from Ben, —

"Keep dark!"

The afternoon session was wearing away, and I begun to lose faith in Joe's prognostications, when at a moment in which no classes were reciting, and all was quiet, there was heard a startling crash, followed by a rattling and rumbling, as though all the long stove-pipes that ran overhead had tumbled down. The scholars all started and looked around.

"Ingersoll," said the master, "go down cellar and see what has caused this disturbance."

Not without much trepidation I proceeded to obey. The cellar was a dark and pokerish place, and as I stumbled about in it I expected every moment to be seized by some hidden intruder. As my eyes adapted themselves to the dim light, I peered cautiously about, but saw nothing save a pile of old, disused stove-pipe, lying innocently in the middle of the floor. Returning above ground, I reported nobody in the cellar.

The words had scarcely passed my lips when rattlety-bang! came another clashing of the dead stove-pipes, as though they were all dancing a hornpipe over the cellar floor. The master eyed me sternly and exclaimed, —

"Come down stairs with me, sir!" Down we went, I taking care to fall into the rear. Nothing was to be seen save the bewitched stove-pipes, demurely

4

huddling together as before. The master examined them carefully, but there seemed to be no life in them, — nothing but old rusty sheet-iron, condemned and useless. He peered about in the corners of the cellar, and behind the wood-piles, but nobody was hidden there.

"Very strange!" muttered the master as we went up the stairs. I began to feel as though *something* was behind me, and this time would rather not have been in the rear.

School was dismissed, and on the way home all the boys were talking of the mysterious noises. Ben Hunter said he believed the cellar was haunted; he'd seen something down there that looked like a ghost.

"Well," said Si Sumner, whose turn it was to build the fire next morning, "I'm not going down into a haunted cellar, anyway."

"Don't be afraid, Si," remarked Joe Jameson. "The ghost won't hurt you. He's after old Duck-Legs. I wouldn't wonder if 't was the ghost of some boy he flogged to death long ago."

"I heard tell of a boy that died once after he was flogged," said little Ed Thompson, his eyes sticking out of his head with wonder and awe.

"'T would have been funny if he hadn't," said Ben Hunter, giving a sly look at Joe Jameson.

"Oh, ho!" thought I, "this is *your* game, is it?"

But I said nothing. Strangely enough, it had not before occurred to me to connect the mysterious noises with Joe Jameson's prediction. Now I thought I would wait and see what came of it all.

Next day there was no recurrence of the noises. Si Sumner, when questioned if he had heard anything in the morning, said he brought an armful of wood from home; he did n't go down into the cellar until after the boys had begun to arrive.

Days passed on, and we were beginning to lose faith in the ghost in the cellar, when one forenoon there was a crash and rattle that set us all agog again. Plainly the noise came from the cellar, though when one of the older boys was sent down he reported nobody there and all quiet. The master said nothing, but he looked very grim. At noon, when school was dismissed, it was noticed by some of the boys, who lagged behind, that he did not leave the school-house as usual.

At the afternoon session the school was called to order. The master stood behind his desk and glared over the room. We all felt that something terrible was about to happen, and you might have heard a pin drop.

"Hunter," said the master, "you will come to the desk."

Ben marched down with his customary swagger.

"I understand you have seen a ghost in the cellar!" said the master.

"Something like it," replied Ben, nothing daunted.

"Did it look like this?" continued the master, taking a brick from under his desk and holding it up before Ben's eyes.

"N-no, sir," he replied, a little staggered.

"Well, did you ever see this brick before?"

"Can't say, sir; I've seen a great many bricks, and they all look very much alike." Cool as a cucumber was Ben.

"Did you ever see a brick with a long string tied to it, like this?"

"Y-yes, sir," said Ben, beginning to falter a little again.

"And did the string run down through a hole in the floor under your desk?"

"I believe it did, sir," replied Ben, who with all his faults would not tell a lie.

"And was it your custom to amuse yourself by dropping this brick, by means of this string, down upon the pile of stove-pipe in the cellar?"

Ben could scarcely resist a grin as he replied, "Yes, sir."

"Well, sir, you will go to your seat and remain after school is dismissed."

The secret was out! The mystery was explained!

Ben, as usual, was at the bottom of the mischief. But what would the master do to him? we asked each other, as we went home, leaving him alone in the dread presence. We doubted not that some terrible punishment awaited him, but nothing had Ben to say when we met him next morning.

"Well, Ben, what did the ghost say to you?" inquired Si Sumner, somewhat quizzically.

"He said you were the brave boy who did n't dare to meet him in the cellar!" retorted Ben.

Si looked a little sheepish, and asked no more questions. He was always, after this, a little sensitive about that ghost.

"But, Ben, how did the master find you out?" I asked.

"That was my confounded carelessness. After I had dropped the brick on the stove-pipe I used to draw it up, and tieing the string to a nail in my desk let the brick hang close to the under side of the floor, where, in the darkness of the cellar, nobody would see it. But that day I was called out to recite before I had time to pull the brick up, and when I came back to my seat I forgot it. So the brick remained on the cellar floor among the stove-pipes. At noon Master Gorham went down cellar poking about, and found the brick with the string leading up through a gimlet-hole in the floor to my seat. And that 's how he found out who was the ghost."

Whatever the master said or did to Ben, it had a good effect upon him. He cut up no more pranks in school, and took a high rank in his studies.

How long my school-days seemed! but looking back upon them now, how rapidly they glided away! I can see myself now sitting on the long, hard, backless bench through the sunny afternoons, at times applying myself to my studies, and at times thinking how jolly it would be to go in swimming "back of the Neck." Vacations were then few and short. We had but a fortnight in the year. After "examination day" had passed, when the committee came and heard our recitations, and made their speeches, the master would call us to order, and we all sat upright in our seats, — even long and lank Jim Applebee, who always leaned against the wall in the draft, or back against the desk behind him when in his seat, — and were silent and expectant.

Then the master, standing at his high desk, would make us a little speech about our conduct during the coming vacation, and dismiss us with the hope of seeing us all again at our books when it was over. At the tap of the ruler we marched out in due order, scarcely able to contain ourselves until we reached the vestibule, when, with a whoop and a hurrah, we leaped over the double row of posts and scampered off to our homes.

CHAPTER IV.

THE GLORIOUS FOURTH.

"HARRY," said Si Sumner, one morning in the latter part of June, "how much money have you got for the Fourth of July?"

"A whole dollar," I replied, with something of exultation in my tone.

"How'd you get so much?" inquired Si, with a little spice of envy.

"I earned it going errands."

"Well, I've got a half-dollar, and a big pile of old iron I'm going to sell down at Munks's. I'll bet I'll get a quarter for it."

Old iron was a commodity largely dealt in by the boys of Liberty Street. It brought a cent a pound, and Si had been a diligent collector. He showed me his pile with pride. Among the scraps there was a part of a barbed instrument that looked like a minia-ture harpoon.

"That'll bring a lot," said Si.

On the way to Munks's we met old Jack Groves, the negro stevedore, whose eye caught the harpoon, as we passed, and taking it from the basket he

offered Si ninepence for it. Si declined the offer
with scorn, confident that it would bring more at the
iron dealer's. When the pile was weighed Mr.
Munks said it came to eleven cents.

"Eleven cents!" exclaimed Si. "Why, Jack
Groves offered me ninepence for the harpoon."

"Well, why did n't you take it? It does n't weigh
a pound."

It began to dawn upon Si that he had placed a
wrong estimate on the value of his harpoon and
missed a chance for a good bargain. He looked disconsolate.

"Never mind, Si," said I, wishing to comfort him.
"I 'll tell you what we can do. You 've got a pistol,
and if we sit up all night we can be the first under
old Capt. Potts's window and get that half-dollar he
always gives to the boy who fires the first salute after
midnight."

"Ben Hunter 's going for that; he 's got a gun,"
said Si, still doleful and dubious.

"But he lives a long way from old Potts's, and if
we go and spend the night with Jim Norton we shall
be close by."

Si began to take heart at this, and it was arranged
that we were to steal out of our homes after going
to bed on the night before the Fourth and proceed to
Jim Norton's.

As I was creeping softly down-stairs on that eventful evening, I heard my grandmother saying, in sleepy tones, —

"I don't believe Betsy put the cat out."

But the cat was out, and after a pause and another cautious advance, I, too, was out. The moon was shining brightly, and all was still as I turned into the street and met Si at the appointed corner.

"How did you get out?" I inquired.

"Tumbled out," said Si, with a groan, rubbing his shin as he spoke. "I climbed out of the back window on to the shed, and before I knew it I slipped and went slap off the roof on to the ground."

"Lucky you did n't wake your father."

"I don't see much luck in it," said Si, who was n't given to looking on the bright side of things.

We hurried down the street and found Jim Norton up and dressed, with a lantern dimly burning. His indulgent mother had given him the use of the kitchen, and Jim had arranged that we were to sit up and tell stories until the witching hour of midnight.

Si, however, was more intent on examining into the condition of his scraped shin, and when Jim saw it he benevolently bestirred himself and bound it up in a tallowed rag.

"You are the first fellow wounded, I do believe," said Jim.

Si did n't find much consolation in this cheering remark, and soon disposed himself on a bench for a nap. Jim and I lay down upon a mat, and Jim told how he had camped out in the woods once with his father, and they heard a bear growling in the night. I seemed myself to be camping out on a mountain, and the mountain was a volcano, and presently there was a tremendous eruption; a column of flame shot up to the heavens, and the ground shook beneath me. As I turned to fly from the stream of lava flowing down the mountain-side, Jim Norton shouted in my ear, —

"That's the Bangtown Artillery, and they 've broke two panes of glass in the kitchen window."

The Bangtown Artillery was an organization of young men who felt it to be a patriotic duty to parade the streets on the night before the Fourth, and fire salutes from a six-pounder. They had discharged their piece in front of the house, and so suggested my dream of a volcano.

"Come, boys," said Jim, "it 's ten minutes of twelve, and I 'll bet Ben Hunter is under old Potts's window now."

Si and I rubbed our sleepy eyes and followed Jim into the street. The moon had gone down, but the stars shone brightly. We turned the corner and entered the long street, half-way down which lived

Capt. Potts. As we ran along we kept our eyes on the far end of the street, at which we knew Ben Hunter would enter it. No one was to be seen in the dim starlight, and we hurried along, sure now of being the first on the ground. A minute later, however, we saw a boy enter the street with a gun in his hand.

"That's Ben," said Si, "but we've got the start of him. Now pull for it."

We ran at our topmost speed, Si quite forgetting his lame leg in the heat of the contest; for now Ben had seen us, and, divining our purpose, was rushing down towards us at a break-neck pace. He was a swift runner, and might, perhaps, have reached the captain's doorstep first, spite of our advantage in distance, had he not tripped on the curbstone, at a cross street, and fallen sprawling on the sidewalk. In a moment more we were under the captain's window. Just then the old Second Parish clock struck twelve. Si elevated his pistol and pulled the trigger. To our consternation it missed fire. In his excitement Si had forgotten to cap it. Ben was now on his feet again, hurrying on, though at a hobbling pace. Trembling with excitement, Si scattered the percussion caps over the sidewalk, but at last succeeded in getting one on the nipple, and bang! went the pistol just as Ben was elevating his gun. Bang!

too, went his gun.   Up went the window over our heads, and out came the nightcapped head of weather-beaten old Capt. Potts, shouting in his hoarse voice, —

" Here you are, my hearties ! "

The half-dollar chinked on the sidewalk, and Si sprang and secured it.

" I 'll pay you for this," cried Ben Hunter, in a high state of exasperation.

" Pay us now," said Si, bravely, we being three to one.   Ben was mad.   This was an act of insubordination on our part.   As the big boy of the neighborhood he ruled tyrannically over the younger fry, and having announced his purpose of securing the old captain's annual donation, it was clearly treason in us to attempt to forestall him.   What might have been the result of a contest on the spot cannot now be known, for the reason that at this moment a crowd of boys approached from various quarters, each of whom had been intent on securing the prize.

" Who got the half-dollar ? " was the universal cry.

" I did," said Si, holding up the coin in sight of all.

" Then, fellows," said good-natured Joe Jameson, " let 's make Si captain, and march around town firing our pistols."

This was agreed to by all except Ben Hunter, who said he was n't going to march in that crowd, and went off with his gun.   When we afterwards marched past his house he shouted after us in derision, —

" Hurrah for Potts's pensioners ! "

What a gunpowdery night was that ! All the youth of Landsport were in the streets, each intent on making as much noise as possible. The roar of the Bangtown six-pounder was succeeded at intervals by the rattle of musketry, the popping of pistols, and the snapping of Chinese fire-crackers. Bang ! went the cannon under the window of some startled sleeper, who, turning uneasily in his bed, muttered an oath perhaps, and dozed off again, only to be awakened by a volley of musketry, the solitary crack of a pistol, or the long rattle of a whole bunch of fire-crackers ignited in an empty barrel. The good people of Landsport were patriotic and tolerant of gunpowder and noise on the glorious Fourth.

The air grew sulphurous and heavy with smoke As the gray of the morning came on, how weird was the aspect of the streets to us sleepy and smoke-begrimed boys as we still went marching on, popping the few pistols we could muster among us ! In the dim twilight of that unaccustomed hour, even familiar objects looked strange to our eyes. The alternation of the uproar with the silence of solitary streets, the unrecognized figures dimly seen in the misty distance, proving on approach to be old acquaintances, but still looking strange and unlike themselves ; the sudden flash and roar from some dark and unsuspected nook, — all combined to give a strange fascination to the scene.

But when at sunrise the bells rang out a merry peal, and the cannon at the arsenal belched forth a national salute, the scene suddenly changed, and we began to have thoughts of home and breakfast. As I was turning into Liberty Street I met little Ed Thompson coming out of Cross Street, where he lived. "O Harry!" said he, "you ought to have been down at my house this morning. Hay-Bag Ross came over to help me fire my cannon, and Tom Sawyer and Bill Jones came with them. And don't you think Tom set his powder down all open, and Hay-Bag threw a match down after he had touched off the cannon, and the gunpowder went off, and flashed away up to the second-story windows, and woke up father and mother; and you ought to have seen Hay-Bag jumping around with his eyebrows singed off, and crying out, 'Oh, my new trousers!' and Tom and Bill leaping over the fence, and father sticking his head out of the window and scolding us, and me a running out of the yard! The powder was all burnt up, and Hay-Bag 'll catch it for scorching his new trousers, and he's got to stay in the house all day because his eyebrows are all singed off!"

True enough, poor Hay-Bag was not visible for the day, nor for a week after, and when he did again appear Ben Hunter said he looked like a singed cat.

As the morning advanced the streets grew lively with the incoming crowd of sight-seers. How brightly the sun shone! What a holiday air pervaded all things! Never was such a day as this in all the year. We seemed to breathe a different atmosphere. The most familiar objects assumed a new and joyous aspect. The shops where candy and fruit were sold became bowers of evergreen. Rows of spruce-trees were stuck in front of saloons and liquor shops. Stands for the sale of lemonade and spruce-beer were set up along the edge of the sidewalks. Every one wore a smiling face, and all were in their best attire. Troops of bright-faced little girls and boys hurried along, full of eager expectation. Long lines of wagons came in from the country towns, filled with farmers, their wives and children, all bent on seeing the sights and enjoying the rare pleasure of a holiday. Queer old characters, never seen on any other day in the year, began to creep out of obscure streets and by-ways, — little dried-up old women in big old-fashioned bonnets; hobbling old men, wizened and gray, attired in antique garb, came out like forgotten relics of a former generation; here and there a Revolutionary pensioner was recognized in the crowd and hailed with many hearty greetings. Now and then a soldier in gay uniform hurried through the press of people blocking up the sidewalks, and anon a mounted officer trotted past, bearing with great dignity his share of the weighty responsibilities of the day. The crowd all surged toward Market Square, the centre of the town, which was soon filled with an expectant multitude. As I pushed about in the crowd I came upon Tim Bunce.

"O Harry!" cried he, "lend me a ninepence."

"Why, Tim, didn't you have any Fourth-of-July money?"

"Yes, I had a half-dollar, but I've spent it all. I didn't think the day was going to be so long!"

As it was then but eight o'clock in the morning, I wondered when Tim began his day, but could not refuse him the ninepence.

Presently the beating of drums was heard. Volunteer companies marched past. The grand procession was forming. After long waiting it appeared, marching down Main Street. First came the mounted truckmen in clean white frocks, moving heavily on their ponderous steeds; next appeared the uniformed militia companies of the town, with drums beating and colors flying; then came the municipal officers, followed by "distinguished citizens"; "officers of the army and navy," comprising two weather-beaten veterans in rusty uniforms; "citizens of other towns," composed of a long line of farmers, walking two by two, with their whips under their arms; the pageant closing with a miscellaneous crowd of straggling teams.

After marching through the dusty streets for an hour or two, the procession halted and massed in rear of the town hall, from a window of which "the orator of the day" stepped forth upon an extemporized platform, manuscript in hand, and read a long oration in a loud voice and with many emphatic gestures.

We boys mingled with the crowd and sat on the doorsteps and curbstones, and made very free comments on the proceedings.

"What is he talking about?" asked Ed Thompson.

"Oh, don't you hear? He's telling about our Revolutionary fathers and how they whipped the British," replied Jim Norton, who prided himself on his historical knowledge.

"My grandfather fought in the Revolution," said Si Sumner, "and I guess he killed as many as a dozen of the British."

"He don't look as if he ever killed anybody," remarked Jim Norton.

Si was about to resent this imputation on the valor of his ancestor, when the drum beat again, an-

5

nouncing the conclusion of the long oration. Then
the bells began to ring, and the cannon boomed
again, the procession re-formed and marched down
Union Wharf to the Hay Magazine, a very long building where tables were spread, at which the weary and
dusty crowd took seats on rough board benches and
began to demolish the rolls and corned beef with a
valor worthy of "the days that tried men's souls."

The scene of the day's festivities now shifted to
the "Hill," which rose at the eastern end of the
town.   On the summit of the Hill stood a red-
shingled observatory, whose purpose was the signal-
ling of ships approaching the port. This observatory,
for some unknown, reason was popularly called the
"monument."   On holidays it was always gay with
long lines of the flags of all nations, extending from
the four flag-staffs on the summit to the ground.

The green slope stretching down from the observatory to the graveyard, where the "rude forefathers
of the hamlet" slept, was the play-ground of the
town.   Here "general muster" was held, and here
the crowd resorted on Independence Day to indulge
in the rude festivities of our one national holiday.
It commanded a wide-extended view of the town
below, of the harbor with its shipping, the opposite
shore of the "Cape," and the ocean beyond.

How stirring was the scene on Independence Day!

The military that had done escort duty in the fore-noon came marching up the deep cut which Congress Street then made in the ascent of the hill, with drums beating and banners flying. They marched and coun-termarched, they deployed and wheeled and charged, in long-extended, wavering line, their bayonets glit-tering in the sunshine. Their white tents dotted the greensward, and were gay with pennons. The offi-cers dined in the big *marquee*, and we boys stood at the openings in the canvas and listened to the toasts and the cheers. As the name of each State was toasted, the roar of a six-pounder mingled with the sound of cheers. Those were patriotic days, and some of the nation's brave defenders showed their devotion to their country by the depth of their pota-tions. Old Gen. McGuire stood up, glass in hand, and exclaimed, —

"Gentlemen, we have now come to the last State in the Union." Thereupon an officer who had al-lowed no State to pass unhonored by him, struggled up unsteadily, and leaning over the table said, —

"Sheneral, is n't there another little State, some-wheres?"

Then there were "the flying horses," on which for five cents we rode until we were dizzy. Fire-crackers were snapping at our feet at every step, while boys with an eye to business were shouting, —

"Crackers! five for a cent!" Venders of cooling beverages were crying, —

"Here's your lemonade, cold as ice can make it!" Jimmy Hall, the English chimney-sweep, at his candy stand was shouting after each sale, as he rattled the money between his hands, —

"Sold the candy, got the money! sold the candy, got the money!"

Old Johnny Avery was singing Revolutionary songs in a cracked voice, while the by-standers tossed pennies into his cap. Then there was the wonderful peep show, exhibited by a dark, outlandish-looking man, speaking with a foreign accent, who, as he pulled the string that shifted the scenes in his box, cried out, —

"The Kensington Palace and gyardens!"

But the centre of attraction was the long line of canvas-covered booths, in which were made tempting displays of gingerbread, eggnog, candies, and fruit.

"Come, boys," said Si Sumner, "I'm going to stand treat with that half-dollar I got of old Potts."

Nothing loath, we all followed Si into one of the larger booths, where tables were provided for the accommodation of hungry customers.

"What shall we have, boys?" said Si, with the grand air which became the magnificent provider of the feast.

"Pie!"

"Lemonade!"

"Gingerbread!"

"Spruce beer!"

"Nuts and candy!"

All cried together, and Si gave his orders accordingly. What a feast was that, and how jolly we all were as we sat at the tables looking out upon the lively scene before us! When our hunger was somewhat appeased, Joe Jameson rose and said, —

"Boys, I give you the health of old Capt. Potts, and long may he live!"

This was received with loud cheers and thumpings of the table. We had not listened at the door of the marquee for nothing. Jim Norton jumped up and cried out, —

"Here's bad luck to Ben Hun —"

He stopped short as he saw Ben's scowling face looking in at the front of the booth. Ben's appearance on the scene threw a damper on our festivities, but he went as suddenly as he came, and we were about to resume our festive cheer when loud shouts, mingled with oaths and the rush of many feet, were heard. Before we could learn the cause of the tumult, a crowd of trampling, fighting, half-drunken men rushed against the side of the booth, the canvas covering was quickly torn off, the struggling mass was upon us, the tables were overturned, some of us were thrown to the ground in the scramble that ensued, and all were glad to struggle out of the crowd as fast as possible.

The shades of evening were beginning to fall, and the keepers of the booths were hurriedly taking down their temporary structures in anticipation of the drunken rows which usually followed the free use of liquors on a holiday. Fights took place between tipsy champions, and gangs of rowdies roamed about demolishing all booths that were not well defended. We scattered down the hill on our way home, and presently I overtook Tim Bunce, who cried out, —

"Ben Hunter paid yer off, after all, did n't he?"

"How so?" I asked.

"Why, did n't yer know he brought that gang down upon your booth? I saw him do it. There was a lot of drunken fellows chasing a nigger from Sandy Holler, and he ran among the booths, and just then Ben ran out and shouted, 'This way! this way!' And he led 'em right down on to your booth. But, my, was n't old Johnson mad?"

"So Ben is still at the bottom of the mischief," was my reflection, as I turned in home, well content to seek the bed I had been so eager to desert the previous night.

CHAPTER V.

HOW JIM TRUMAN LOST HIS ARM.

BILL TRUMAN lived in a small house near the twine factory. It stood close upon the street, which since its erection had been raised to a level with the lower-story windows. The old house seemed to be settling into the earth, going down with the fortunes of its occupants; for Bill's father, Mr. James Truman, commonly called Jim Truman, had seen better days. "Yes, boys," he would say, in his confidential moments, "I'm not what I used to be. I've seen the time when you would n't catch me working for old Frye for a dollar a day."

Jim worked in the twine factory, an establishment of great interest to us boys, since we were seldom permitted to enter it. One day in the autumn following the events of the last chapter, Bill Truman asked Joe Jameson and myself to go with him to the factory where he was employed in turning a wheel. Glad enough to gain entrance to this mysterious building, which was so long it seemed to have no end, and whose many windows were always blinking at us when we played "I spy" in the lumber-yard, we readily as-sented, and soon found ourselves standing at the upper end of a long, narrow apartment which stretched away into a dim and dusty distance. Here stood the wheel which Bill was employed to turn, while Mr. Frye, with a bunch of tow at his waist, walked backward down a long aisle, spinning an ever-lengthening line as he went. Bill turned, and Mr. Frye twisted with thumb and finger, and so the twine grew until it carried Mr. Frye so far away we wondered if he would ever get back again.

After watching this operation for a time, and giving Bill an occasional "spell" at the wheel, we turned our attention to his father's proceedings. Mr. Truman was hatchelling flax. Taking a quantity of this material in his hand he threw it over some long, sharp iron teeth which stood upright in a board and drew it through them until it was combed out clean and straight. This process was preparatory to the twisting of the twine. Truman had but one hand, having lost his left arm above the elbow. This made him an object of much interest to us boys, who looked with some awe on the empty sleeve, the end of which was sewed into the pocket of his short jacket. I had often wondered what had become of that missing arm. There were whispers among the boys that Jim had been in the wars, and had lost his arm in a desperate encounter with the enemy. We looked upon him as a good deal of a hero, though at times his acts did not entirely sustain that character. These occasions were always immediately after he got the pension paid him by government.

As we watched him swinging his right arm while hatchelling the flax, an overpowering impulse seized upon Joe Jameson, and before he had time to consider the audacity of the question he blurted out,—

"Mr. Truman, won't you tell us how you lost your arm?"

"Ah, my boy, that's a long story."

"Please to tell us," we both pleaded in a breath.

"I'm too busy now," said Truman, thrashing away at the flax. "Some other time perhaps I will."

"Come, father," said Bill, "you know you got your pension to-day, and you promised me a candy scrape when you got the money. Let's have it to-night, and then you can tell the boys the whole story."

Mr. Truman paused in his labor and wiped his brow on his shirt-sleeve. "I don't remember such a promise," he said, dubiously, and our anticipations fell to zero; but he added, "you've worked pretty well, Bill, the last fortnight, and I don't mind giving you a treat."

"Hurrah!" cried Bill, applying himself to the crank with renewed vigor, while Joe and I rubbed our hands in glee.

That evening an eager company of boys gathered in the low kitchen of the little house under the sidewalk. A bright fire was blazing in the open fireplace, and on the crane hung an iron pot, into which Bill had poured as much as two quarts of molasses.

"What a gob that 'll make!" cried Tim Bunce, highly delighted at the lavishness of the treat.

We all sat around the fire in a high state of expectancy, while Bill, who claimed to be a "dabster" at making molasses candy, stirred the contents of the pot to prevent its "catching" on the bottom. The molasses boiled and bubbled, and rose to the mouth of the pot, out of which it was only prevented from boiling by frequent stirrings. After much tasting all around from a long-handled spoon, the candy was pronounced "done," the great crane was swung out and the pot carefully lifted from it.

"I 'll butter the platter," said Si Sumner, busily applying himself to the task with a lump of butter kindly furnished by Bill's grandmother.

It was decided that the candy should be set to cool, before "working," on a bench outside the back door.

Just then Mr. Truman, who had donned his best coat in honor of the occasion, made his appearance on the scene, and was loudly welcomed.

Mr. Truman was in a hilarious state of mind, as

he usually was when he got his pension money, though neither lasted long.

"Now, Mr. Truman," said Joe Jameson, "please tell us how you lost your arm."

"Yes, father," said Bill, "you can tell the story while the candy is cooling."

"Boys," began Mr. Truman, "you don't remember the war of 1812. I do. I was a lad not much older than some of you, then. It was pretty hard times here in Landsport for a while, I tell ye. When they put the embargo on, everything stopped, and people who were well off before were glad to go to the soup-house to get something to eat.

"After the fighting began on the sea, some of our folks thought they might as well have a hand in it, and old Jake McNaughton and others fitted out a privateer. One day I went down on to Long Wharf just as they was taking her cannon aboard. Capt. Jim Reed, he stood on the deck of the 'Saucy Jack,' — that was the name of the privateer, — and seeing me, he called out, —

"'My boy, don't you want to make your fortune?'

"I said I did n't know. For ye see I had n't much idee about this privateering, though I found out afterwards that some of the owners, and the crew, too, did make a pile of money out of it. Well, Capt. Reed he told me that if I 'd ship with him I 'd get a lot o' prize money. He wanted a boy about my size for powder-monkey. Mother said I should n't go, but father said times was hard, and I might as well be doing something.

"Well, the upshot of it was I shipped aboard the 'Saucy Jack.' She carried eight guns and a crew of one hundred men. They was most all Landsport boys, and all of 'em but me had been to sea afore. I was pretty seasick at the first on it, and wished I had n't shipped, I tell ye, but when I got my sea legs on I could eat all afore me.

"One day we saw a sail and soon overhauled her, for the 'Saucy Jack' was a fast sailer. The captain said he 'd lay us alongside and board her. So we got into close quarters, when, hang me if she did n't open a heavy fire on us. It was a British man-o'-war in disguise! I tell you we jumped around pretty lively when we found that out. We had two men killed afore we knew what was the matter with us. The captain, he swore like blazes, and we began to claw off as fast as we could. But the wind was light and the frigate was bearing down upon us, when the captain cried, 'Out with the sweeps!' And we took to the long oars and pulled away for dear life. Still we did n't gain much, so the captain ordered out the boats, and they carried out kedges, and then all hands took hold of the line and pulled her up to one of 'em, while the boat carried another kedge ahead. In this way we began to crawl away from the frigate, but when she saw what we was up to, she sent out her boats and began to play the same game with kedges.

"Then it was nip and tuck, I tell ye! I thought the 'Saucy Jack' was a goner, but her time had n't come jest yet. Pretty soon the frigate see we was slipping away from her, so she opened on us with her bow chasers, and the way the splinters flew about my ears was a caution. My heart went down to the bottom of my boots, but pretty soon I got so hot serving powder to our guns that I never thought about the danger. Just then smash came a shot on board, and down I went on the deck."

"And your arm was shot off!" cried Jim Norton, who had been listening with open-mouthed attention.

"Not so fast, my lad," said Truman, while all the boys cried out to Jim to hush up, and we drew still closer around the hero of the hour.

"No, I was only knocked down by the wind of the ball. Ye see a cannon-ball makes a big hole in the air, and the wind rushes in after it powerful. I was soon on my feet again, and by this time a light breeze had sprung up, and we soon left the frigate behind. But it was a narrow escape, I tell ye. Well, we cruised about for a week, after that, without falling in with anything, and the captain began to get rather down in the mouth at our bad luck, when one day a whole fleet of merchantmen hove in sight under convoy of a frigate, and the captain swore he'd capture one of them merchantmen in spite of the frigate. So we gave chase as bold as a lion, and when the frigate began to chase us, we turned tail and led her a long chase till night fell, when we slipped away from her in the darkness.

"Next morning there was the merchant ships all drawn up as if in order of battle. We pounced down on 'em pretty quick, I tell ye; sailed slap right through their line, give 'em broadsides right and left, and then raked 'em fore and aft, till four of 'em struck their colors. We could have taken more of 'em if we had had men enough to man 'em. But perhaps you want to know where the frigate was all this time. Why, she was cruising about after us! that was the joke of it.

"Our next brush with the enemy wasn't so much of a joke. We'd been a scuddin' along all night before a stiff breeze, and at daylight a sail hove in sight low down on the horizon. The captain he went for everything he saw, but when we got a better view of the stranger he didn't like the looks on her. Fact is, it was a British frigate, and she was a bearing right down on us. We spread all sail, but the frigate

had the weather-gauge of us, and she was n't so clumsy
as most of the British men-o'-war was in them days.
She kept a gaining on us, though we spread every rag
of canvas. It was pretty exciting for a time, I tell
ye. The 'Saucy Jack' was n't no slow-goer, but
she 'd met her match this time.

"'Boys,' said Capt. Reed, 'we ain't a going to a
British prison, not yet. Give her a shot.'

"The shot fell short, and only splashed up the sea,
but it brought out a shot from the frigate that did
for us. Crash went our main-topmast, carrying everything by the board. Before we could clear away the
wreck another shot raked our deck, fore and aft,
and killed three men. Things began to look pretty
serious then, I tell ye. The captain he was hit by a
splinter, but he would n't go below. We give the
frigate a broadside, and then she poured one into us
that came nigh on to sinking us. Our flag was shot
away, and the frigate hailed us and asked if we 'd sur-
rendered. The captain tried to sing out "No!" but
he was too weak from loss of blood to be heard, and
the frigate sent her boats aboard and took possession.

"The British leftenant said we was a prize to his
Majesty's ship 'Swaggerer.' And a swaggerer she
was, too, and all her officers, for that matter. They
bullied us the worst kind. They put a prize crew
aboard the 'Saucy Jack,' and sent our crew aboard

the frigate. Then we was all drawed up in a line to see if there was any Britishers among us. You see, the British they claimed the right to take their sailors out of our ships whenever they found 'em, and they was n't very partic'lar to make sure o getting the right man, neither. I had my protection papers, and they did n't say nothing to me, but some of our crew did n't have any papers, and they put 'em in irons. The frigate put into Portsmouth, England, and we was sent to Dartmoor prison. It was a gloomy place, on high land, where it rained or snowed the whole year round, and was cold enough to wear a great-coat the whole time. There was more than five thousand prisoners there and we had a pretty hard time of it, for they did n't give us none too much to eat.

"I s'pose I'd been there pretty nigh a year when one day a lot of us was playing ball in the prison yard. I tossed the ball to the man at the bat, and he knocked it over the prison wall. We'd done this afore, and the sentry always throwed it back to us. This day it happened there was a surly fellow on guard, and when we sung out for him to throw the ball over he swore he would n't. Jack Carson called out, 'If you don't throw it over we'll dig a hole through the wall and get it.'

"The sentry, he told us to come on if we wanted

to, and so, just for fun, we all made a rush for the wall and began digging a hole in the brick work. The officer on duty he saw the rush, and ordered us back into the yard; and then Capt. Shortland marched his troops into the yard, and while we was all standing there waiting for what was to come next, he ordered the soldiers to fire on us. We never expected he was going to shoot us, and when the men began to fall the rest of us ran to get shelter. I tried to get behind a gate, but just as I reached it I felt a sharp pain in my arm, and it fell by my side. When it was all over, and the doc tor came to look at me, he said the bone was shat. tered and they would have to cut it off; and that's the way I lost my arm, boys."

We all drew a long breath, and Si Sumner said, "Why did n't you prisoners rise on the guard and kill the whole of 'em?"

"Fact is, we wanted to bad enough, but we had n't no weapons. But you ought to have heard the men yelling and swearing at old Shortland. They fright-ened him so he never dared to show his head again while they was in the prison. The British govern-ment, they said it was all a mistake, but there was no mistake that Shortland was a coward and a brute. There was seven men killed and thirty-eight wounded, — and all for nothing."

6

"I guess that candy's cool enough by this time," said Bill. "Fetch it in, Tim."

We had forgotten all about the candy while listening to Truman's story, but now our interest in it suddenly revived, and we were all ready for the treat, when Tim burst into the room, his red hair standing up like porcupine quills, and gasped out, —

"The candy's gone!"

"Gone!" cried we all, in consternation.

"Yes," said Tim, "I can't find it nowhere."

"Some of the fellows have hid it, I guess," said Bill, as we all rushed out of the room in search of our lost treat.

It was gone, sure enough, platter and all. We searched all about the premises, but no trace of it was discovered. A deep gloom fell upon us.

"This is plaguy mean," said Si Sumner; "do you s'pose Ben Hunter stole it?"

"Like as not," replied Bill; "he wasn't invited."

"Boys," said his father, thrusting his hand into his pocket with an air of great munificence, "you sha'n't lose your treat. Here's a silver half-dollar. Go over to Delande's and buy some candy."

We were profuse in our thanks, to which Truman replied, with a wave of his hand, "You're welcome, boys, welcome." He was always as rich as a Jew the day he got his pension money. We adjourned to Delande's confectionery shop, where the half-dollar was invested in long sticks of molasses candy, each with a big nob at one end.

By this time the hour had grown late, and as Jim Norton lived at the lower end of the town some of us volunteered to accompany him part of the way home. The moon was shining brightly, and as we walked the quiet streets a spirit of bravado and mischief, partly incited, perhaps, by the warlike deeds of which we had heard, and partly by the animal spirits of youth, took possession of us. We felt like taking the freedom of the town in defiance of the two ancient watchmen who were supposed to be somewhere guarding its hours of slumber.

At the corner of Union and Middle Streets we came upon a pile of very large grindstones lying on the edge of the sidewalk in front of a shop door. A happy thought struck me.

"Boys," said I, "let's have some fun. Let's set one of these grindstones rolling down the street, and see where it will bring up."

"Agreed!" cried they all; and we immediately began tugging at the topmost stone, which we found a heavier customer than we had supposed it would be. With our united strength we were able, after repeated efforts, to push it from the pile and stand it upon its edge. It required great exertion to roll it into the middle of the street, and at one time it came near falling upon Si Sumner. However, we at length got it headed down the steep incline of Union Street, and at the word "Let go, boys," away it went, slowly at first, and then more and more rapidly, until it acquired great speed and momentum.

"See it spin!" cried Tim Bunce, dancing frantically and waving his hat in the air.

I watched it with great interest, and not without a secret fear that mischief might come of it. Presently some inequality in the roadway turned it aside from its direct course. It was now aiming directly for the small wooden house in which old Tom Prince lived. We knew he had died that very day. My heart was in my mouth We all stood silent, watching its course with strained attention, until it went dashing through the low front door of the house, which opened directly upon the sidewalk.

Now it happened that two respectable citizens, in accordance with the custom of the time, were at that moment engaged in taking their toddy to sustain them in the awesome duty of watching the corpse of old Tom Prince. As the tremendous intruder came crashing in upon them they sprang to their feet, and dropping their glasses rushed to the door. One of them afterwards said, in relating the experience of that fearful night, that he thought Satan himself had come to take possession of old Tom, body and all.

As we saw the two faithful watchers emerging hatless from the door, we took to our heels and ran for dear life to our several homes.

For some days after this midnight adventure there were no more quiet, studious, well-behaved boys at home or in school than the party who were guilty of the vagaries of that unlucky grindstone. Every time Mr. Burns, the town crier, rang his bell and made his proclamation at the street corners of an auction sale or a lost child, we trembled with fear lest he should be offering a reward for the detection of those who set that stone in motion. He always bawled himself so hoarse and rattled so hurriedly through the matter in hand that we never knew what he was saying.

Yet with all our fear of detection we had a sort of guilty enjoyment of the fun of the thing. We always laughed when we thought of those two respectable citizens rushing out hatless into the street. Meeting Tim Bunce some days after, he said, in an aside, "Tell you what, Harry, it's no use saying our rolling stone gathered no moss, for did n't it bring old Morse to the door in a hurry?"

The affair made some stir in town. Some expressed the belief that it was the watchmen who set the stone in motion ; the citizens then took turns on the night watch, by way of paying some portion of their taxes, and it was said that the watch were not always exempt from a mischievous disposition, and that many mad pranks were of their commission. Others held that the stone must have fallen off the pile and set out on its travels on its own account. We never contradicted this reasonable supposition, being well content that the stone should bear the whole weight of its transgression.

Withington, the local poet, who used to sell his rhymes about the streets, printed on broadsides, made a song concerning the event, beginning, —

> " Oh, have you heard the news of late,
> How down the street came rolling straight,
>   At midnight's witching hour,
> A mighty stone that found its way
> Where, in death's grasp, our neighbor lay,
>   And ' waked ' him with its power? "

We boys all bought a copy, and I have mine lying by me yet.

But who stole that molasses candy? We never knew. Some months after, Jim Norton, while playing with other boys in one of the old disused distilleries, found an empty platter, which Bill Truman recognized as his father's property. But nothing further came of it. The disappearance of that candy remains a mystery.

CHAPTER VI.

GENERAL MUSTER.

"GOING to general muster?" said Si Sumner, one bright September morning, as we trudged along to school.

"I guess so," was my reply.

"It's going to be out on the plains, and all the companies will be there, and I should n't wonder if there was a sham fight."

"That'll be jolly!"

"I tell you what," continued Si, with the inspiration of a happy thought, "let's get up a company and march out with 'em. It'll be fun."

"Agreed! And Ben Hunter shall be captain."

There was a strong military spirit prevailing in those days, fully shared by the boys of Liberty Street. What holidays were those when "The Blues" or "The Light Infantry" paraded on their anniversaries, and we followed the inspiring music of fife and drum to "the hill" where the tents were pitched and the target practice took place! We boys perched ourselves on the long line of great bowlders which enclosed the field, on the top of the

hill, near "the monument," and watched the pepper-
ing of the target with great enthusiasm. Then the
prizes — usually gold medals or a set of silver
spoons — were bestowed with much ceremony on
those who made the best shots. Nor was the worst
shot overlooked, its unlucky perpetrator being inva·
riably rewarded with a leather medal, accompanied
with remarks more satirical than complimentary.
On one occasion, I remember, the orator who presented the leather medal to the poorest shot of the
Infantry, quoted Ebenezer Eliot's lines, —

"He does well who does his best,
Is he weary — let him rest."

After target practice came the dinner, served in
a big marquee, followed by toasts, the telling of
stories, and the singing of songs. Sometimes the
companies, on these anniversary occasions, would
march out to "Broad's," a famous hostelry in the
suburbs of the town, and celebrate the day with a
grand dinner, the bill of fare including turtle soup,
haddock chowder, the usual meats and "fixings,".
together with a liberal supply of "Volnay," Bur-
gundy, Joli champagne, old Madeira, Port and Cu-
raçoa wines. From these banquetings the brave
troops marched home a little unsteady, sometimes
discharging their muskets as they marched, to the

imminent peril of each other's whiskers and eye-brows.

But the occasion of greatest sport was the annual May training. We boys never failed to absent ourselves from school on these occasions. Then all the companies turned out for inspection, including " the old militia." This latter designation was applied to the ununiformed companies, of which each ward of the city was expected to furnish one. A motley crowd they were! As each .man was compelled to furnish his own arms and equipments, the weapons mustered would have formed an interesting collection in an antiquarian museum. One tall youth came with an old queen's arm ; another appeared with his father's fowling-piece ; a third brought a rifle, and a fourth a blunderbuss. Joe Witham once appeared on the muster ground with an umbrella-stick. When remonstrated with by the angry officer in command, Joe declared that his stick "would open and shut in a way to frighten the stoutest bull, let alone John Bull himself !" ·

When this motley company was marshalled in a long, wavering line, the captain, lieutenants, and en-sign, gorgeously arrayed in blue uniforms with gold stripes down the trousers legs, and with enormous *chapeaus* on their heads, took their positions, and the order was shouted forth, " Shoulder arms !"

Up went the old muskets, fowling-pieces, and blunderbusses, one after the other, presenting a formidable array. The next thing in order was to wheel the line into ranks. This was not accomplished without much confusion and a good deal of swearing on the part of the officers, but being at last effected, the order, " Forward — *march !* " was shouted forth, and away marched the company, with a bobtail of boys, to the muster-field.

Arrived on the ground, the line was again formed, and the company put through the manual of arms, with many awkward blunders and consequent objurgations on the part of the officers. Jonathan Bloodgood, a tall cobbler, who commanded the company from Ward Three, having his company in line in front of a board fence, drew his " cheese-knife " as he called his sword, and shouted the order to " Charge bagnets ! "

Away went the intrepid troop, and down went the fence, with not a few of the men prostrate among the ruins. Jonathan's company was the only one that reported a list of wounded on that eventful day. Truman Osgood, a short, stumpy private, could never keep step.

" Put your right foot forward," said the officer in command.

" I can't tell which is which," replied Truman.

"Don't you know your left foot from your right? Then I'll mark it for you."

Procuring a piece of chalk, the officer made a broad white cross on Truman's left shoe, which enabled that sturdy youth to keep step with his comrades.

Much rivalry existed between the "volunteer companies" of those days. The Blues were jealous of the Light Infantry, and the animosity between the two companies led to some exciting encounters on the annual parades. One of the companies would sometimes form a line across the street, in advance of the other, and thus block the way, compelling a halt. Then would follow manœuvring to obstruct the advance, until the men got warmed up, when collisions would occur, with rough usage on both sides.

On one occasion the Light Infantry achieved a great triumph over the Blues. The latter company had got possession of a new movement, which was secretly practised in the armory with the intention of bringing it out at May training, to the astonishment and chagrin of the Light Infantry; a member of the Infantry got wind of this, and, secreting himself in a position in the armory adjoining that of the Blues which enabled him to observe the movement, after gaining a thorough comprehension of it, hurried away to the cobbler's shop of a comrade, where he reproduced the movement by cutting it out on a piece of leather.   Notifications were immediately sent out, the members of the Infantry assembled in their armory that evening, and by diligent practice soon acquired proficiency in the new movement.   Every member was sworn to profound secrecy, the intention being to forestall the Blues in the public exhibition of their own evolution.

May training came two days later, and the Infantry were careful to be the first on the march.   Arriving at the corner of Middle and Exchange Streets, they drew up in line and awaited the approach of the Blues.   As the latter marched past, the orders were shouted out by the captain of the Infantry, and his company went through the evolution which the Blues had so secretly cherished as their own exclusive property.   The chagrin and exasperation of the Blues was highly enjoyed by the Infantry, and the affair did not tend to promote good feeling between the two companies.

Ben Hunter readily fell into the plan of forming a military company.   Ben was of a martial spirit and easily assumed a tone of command.

"Boys," said he, as we gathered one afternoon in the coach-house of the stage company's stable, " you must be armed with spears, wooden swords won't do ; we can cut some poles and get the spear-heads at

Cross's tin shop. The officers must carry swords, tin ones, if they can't do better, but I shall carry my grandfather's sword, with which he fought at Bunker Hill."

We all looked at Ben with admiration, and when at the muster in the lumber-yard he buckled on the sword of his grandfather, the scabbard of which, by the way, trailed upon the ground, he was the hero of the hour.

After much drilling in the seclusion of the lumber-yard, it was agreed that we should make a public parade. Out we marched boldly into Liberty Street; although I confess that as first lieutenant I was a little nervous about the prominent appearance I was about to make in the eyes of the public.

As we turned into Cross Street we encountered Ross's long truck extended across the street. Here was a barricade to be carried at the point of the bay-onet, or rather spear-head.

"Charge!" cried Capt. Hunter.

But as he gallantly rushed forward to lead his men to the encounter, the scabbard of his grandfather's sword got between his legs and tripped him up. He fell sprawling across the truck, and just then the horse attached to it, known as "Old Sleepy Davy," suddenly woke up, and wheeling around, brought down the long truck, with the sweep of an alligator's tail, upon the

whole company, who fell to the ground by the score,
— or rather the half-score, as there were but ten privates and three officers. Such a scrambling and
shouting as ensued! Capt. Ben was first upon his
feet, giving the order to " Fall into line."

"We've had one fall, a'ready," said Tim Bunce,
rubbing his shins, with his customary grimace, " and
that's enough for me."

So thought we all of us, and the company was then
and there dismissed for the day. The list of casual-
ties comprised three shins barked, one arm bruised,
and two spears broken. As this was our first engagement, it was thought the company highly distinguished
itself. The enemy — comprising " Sleepy Davy"
and Hay-bag Ross, the latter of whom appeared upon
the scene at the critical moment — was captured,
horse, foot, and dragoons, and driven off in triumph to
their customary stand at the junction of Liberty and
Middle Streets, where " Sleepy Davy" soon fell into
his habitual doze.

In view of possible encounters on the road, and
more especially in consideration of the spiteful derision of our hereditary enemies, the Hog-Towners, it
was unanimously voted not to march to the muster-
field, but to assemble on the ground, "armed and
equipped as the law directs."

On the morning of the eventful day the members

of the company were therefore at liberty to proceed to the headquarters of the military having their armories in the third story of the town-hall in Market Square. This was a favorite resort of us boys whenever there was a training. Each of the four uniformed companies, the Blues, the Light Infantry, the Artillery, and the Rifle Corps, had an armory in one of the four corners of the open loft, the centre of which was used as a drill-room. These armories, in addition to the racks filled with brightly burnished swords and guns, were adorned with highly colored engravings of military heroes, upon which we gazed with great awe and admiration.

What a scene of bustle and admired confusion was the drill-room on the morning of general muster! Soldiers in gay uniforms donning their equipments, officers bustling about with an air of great importance, the calling of the roll, the word of command, the tap of the drum, and the imposing march down the grand staircase into the street!

Then the regimental line was formed, the "old militia" — the various companies of which had assembled in their several wards — forming the extreme left. The regimental officers dashed about on horseback, the companies wheeled into columns, and the regiment began the march up Main Street towards the muster-ground on "the plains."

What a motley array it presented, to be sure! Each of the uniformed companies was arrayed in an entirely different uniform, one wearing huge bear-skin caps, another cloth caps with tall nodding plumes, while the ununiformed companies appeared in rusty garb of every-day wear. Nearly every company had some sort of music, and each band played a different tune. Nevertheless, it was a stirring and a glorious pageant! The street was lined with spectators, women and children flocked to doors and windows to gaze upon the unwonted spectacle, and we boys followed after in an admiring crowd.

The march to the plains was over a dusty road, calling for frequent halts and much consumption of water, not unmingled with something stronger. Arrived at the scene of the muster, a level, grass-grown plain, in the adjoining town of Eastbrook, the regiment was drawn up in a line, other companies from neighboring towns falling into their places. Among these was the Duck Pond Light Infantry, in white pantaloons and blue coats, and the Eastbrook Artillery, numbering fifteen privates. The captain of the artillery asked Capt. Bradford, of the Landsport Artillery, to loan him a file of men to eke out his scanty ranks, but that officer thought it better that each should command his own men. These com-

panies came upon the ground to the stirring music of
fife and drum and with a grand military air.

Uncle Bishop now appeared upon the scene bearing a huge leathern bag filled with silver half-dollars,
and passing along the line dealt out a silver half-
dollar to each private as pay for the day's service.
Thus munificent was the State! The regiment now
marched to a neighboring field, where tents were
pitched and evolutions were to be performed.

Capt. Hunter thought it high time to call his company together. We had come upon the ground in a
somewhat straggling manner, Jim Norton limping in
the rear because of a wound received in the action
with "Sleepy Davy." The roll being called, every
boy drew his spear-head from his pocket and screwed
it upon its pole. Being thus armed and equipped,
the line was formed, and we marched away to the
muster-field, Capt. Hunter flourishing his grandfather's sword in a most heroic manner. After much
marching and countermarching, the company was
drawn up for drill in double line.

"Rear rank, open order," shouted Capt. Hunter.

The rear rank stepped backward, but in doing so
unfortunately stumbled over a tub of lemonade which
had been prepared for the refreshment of the Eastbrook Artillery, after the arduous duties of the day.
Tim Bunce and little Ned Thompson fell slap into

the tub, causing a great overflow and waste of the
grateful beverage. Thereupon the commissary of
the Artillery rushed out of a tent near by, and seizing
Tim with one hand and Ned with the other, not only
rescued them from all danger of drowning, but
knocked their heads together in so vigorous a manner that they were at once restored to a very lively
consciousness of their perilous situation.

"To the rescue, boys," shouted Capt. Hunter,
whereupon a half-dozen of us fell upon the commissary and soon rolled him upon the ground. In the
melee the tub of lemonade was capsized, and the
commissary got more than his share of the refreshing
beverage. As he rose dripping from the ground,
clutching a half-lemon in each hand, and with vengeance in his eye, several of his comrades came running to his rescue. "The Liberty Street Lancers,"
finding the enemy likely to be too strong for them,
thereupon beat a hasty retreat.

"Wring me out, boys," said Tim Bunce, as we
gathered in a sunny corner of the field, whither we had
retired for the purpose of drying our drenched garments; "wring me out, and you can all have a swig!"

"Men," cried Capt. Hunter, with an air that commanded attention, "this is our second engagement,
and I move it be known in our annals as the Battle
of the Tub."

"Seems to me it was more like a naval engagement," said Tim. "I am sure I swam ashore."

"I wish some of the lemonade in my shoe had gone down my throat," added little Ned Thompson, dolefully ; "I 'm getting awful dry."

"And I 'm getting hungry, too," said Joe Jameson. "And that reminds me, boys, that my uncle keeps the tavern at the corner, where all the officers are going to dine to-day, and he has invited me to get my dinner there. You come on, and I 'll chuck you out something to eat."

Nothing loath, we all accepted Joe's second-hand invitation, and sending him forward as a forager, we advanced upon the tavern in good order. Joe entered the house boldly, and after waiting some time we saw his head appearing from an upper window. Beckoning to us, he began dropping down rolls and slices of beef, which we caught in our caps.

While thus busily engaged, and just as Joe had said, "Here you go again, boys," we saw his head suddenly disappear from the window with a jerk, while a gruff voice exclaimed, —

"What does all this mean, you young scamp?"

Rightly concluding that Joe's uncle did not approve of his foraging operations, we withdrew to a safe distance and awaited his appearance. He came out presently, looking rather crestfallen, but said, —

"Never mind, boys, I've got a lot of grub in my pockets."

Just then a familiar voice cried, "Here's your gingerbread and spruce beer." And turning, we beheld Hay-bag Ross presiding at a booth with great activity. We immediately resolved to patronize home enterprise, and soon made a great reduction in Hay-bag's stock of edibles.

It was now time for the sham fight, with which the day's manœuvres were to end, and we therefore proceeded to the muster-field to witness the exciting scene.

"Tell you what, fellers," said Jim Norton, "this is going to be a regular battle. My cousin, Sam Brown, is in the Light Infantry, and he says they're going to fire with balls."

"You must be a greeny if you believe that," said Capt. Hunter; "why, somebody'd get killed."

A discharge of musketry hurried us on, and we found the regiment drawn up in two long, wavering lines, alternately popping away at each other. The firing was a little irregular; first, a simultaneous discharge of muskets, and then the laggards came popping along, one after the other, like the sputtering of a half-spent fire.

Presently an advance was ordered by the commander of the Americans, but the captain of the

Duck Pond Light Infantry stood gawking about, entirely oblivious of the order. As his company occupied the extreme left, and the line moved on to the right, he and his company were left detached and exposed to the enemy's charge. Observing his danger, Adjutant Jones dashed down upon him with an angry order, but he came too late. The enemy had seen the opportunity, and moving a detachment forward on the double quick, completely surrounded the surprised Duck-Ponders, who found themselves prisoners of war before they knew that an advance had been ordered.

Enraged at this blunder, Adjutant Jones detached two companies and came down to the rescue. A hand-to-hand conflict ensued, and the remainder of the contending forces, observing the critical state of affairs, broke ranks and came helter-skelter to join in the fray. There was much clubbing of muskets, knocking down, and dragging out, while the officers, dashing about the combatants on horseback, yelled themselves hoarse in issuing commands that were wholly unheeded.

We boys looked on in excited amusement. Capt. Hunter was half disposed to order a charge by the Liberty Street Lancers, but he prudently forbore.

"Did n't I tell you it was going to be a real battle?" said Jim Norton.

"I should say it was more like a drunken row," replied Joe Jameson, who had been very sober since the admonition administered by his uncle.

Truth to tell, the liquor drank by the soldiers during the day was, in large degree, the animating spirit of the conflict.

By this time the officers had succeeded in disentangling the excited combatants. The line was formed again, the regiment dismissed with a reprimand, and the Landsport companies marched back to town, we boys following as best our weary legs would let us.

CHAPTER VII.

THE LIBERTY STREET LANCERS GO INTO WINTER QUARTERS.

THERE was a great fall of snow early in the winter succeeding the autumn of the memorable sham fight on the plains. The Liberty Street Lancers had kept up their organization, meeting on stated occasions in the lumber-yard for drill in the manual of arms. On one occasion they had made a grand parade through the town, Joe Jameson, as ensign, proudly bearing a banner wrought by the fair hands of the sisters and cousins of the members.

It was on this parade that they encountered a band of their hereditary enemies, the Hog-Towners. Now just who the Hog-Towners were, or in what porcine portion of the town they abode, was never quite clear to my apprehension. There was a mystery about them like that which surrounded the hordes of barbarians who came down from the north on the cities of the ancient Romans. I only knew that they came from up-town somewhere, that there was an ancient grudge between them and the Liberty Street boys, and that they were accustomed to make predatory raids on the possessions of the latter. When a Liberty-Streeter met a Hog-Towner, fierce scowls were exchanged, leading sometimes to fiercer words, and not unfrequently to hot encounters.

On this particular occasion, the Hog-Towners began the fray by discharging a volley of stones at the company as it marched along with gallant bearing. This was immediately resented by a charge upon the enemy, Capt. Hunter leading the attack with the sword of his grandfather. The enemy were put to inglorious flight, skulking away behind fences, from which safe covert they returned a few scattering shots. The Lancers marched proudly off the field in good order. We heard later, from scouts who ventured into the outskirts of the unexplored Hog-Town, that they had sworn vengeance against us, but we valorously laughed them to scorn.

Meantime, as I have said, winter came on, with abundance of snow, covering the land with a great white mantle, peopling our accustomed haunts with fantastic forms. The stacks of hoop-poles in the lumber-yard loomed up like Arctic giants, and seemed to be reaching out long arms to seize us. The piles of boards took on the aspect of snowy mountain ranges. Si Sumner, who had been reading a book of European travel, named them the Alps, one ofty pile receiving the designation of Mont Blanc.

We boys fairly revelled in the snow. We could not understand what our fathers and mothers were complaining about when they grumbled at its depth. Such fun it was to shovel paths, to tunnel through the drifts, to climb high fences and leap into the depths, to lose ourselves in them and come up again, all snowy white and rosy red ; to tumble each other over in the soft bed, to wallow in it, to toss great masses at each other, to make snow-balls, and engage in a regular pitched battle. Ah ! how exhilarating is the snow to youthful blood ! How the spirits rise at the thought of wrestling with it ; how it excites to the encounter with wintry winds, with bitter cold, and how it strengthens the courage and toughens the frame for the greater encounters of life which are sure to come ! But, ah me ! how the very sight of it sends a shiver down the backs of us rheumatic old fellows who have had our day !

"Boys !" said Ben Hunter, one day, after a lively game of snowballing, "it's time the Lancers went into winter quarters. We must build a fort."

"Agreed !" cried we all, and forthwith a council was held to determine plans and location. It was agreed that the lumber-yard should be the scene of operations, and that a detail of men should work at the construction of the fort on half-holidays. Si Sumner, whose father was a carpenter and builder, was appointed master workman, and he immediately proceeded to lay out the plan of the fort in the form of a square.   Capt. Hunter said there must be bastions and bomb-proofs, but Si made some demur to this.

Meantime the snow was cleared away from a level spot and great blocks of the damp material were squared and shaped for the walls.   Joe Jameson proposed that we should pour water on them and let it freeze over night, to make the blocks solid. This was done, and soon the walls began to rise and assume a formidable appearance.

Ben Hunter insisted that we must have a powder magazine in which to store our ammunition, said ammunition consisting of a heap of well-hardened snow-balls.   There was much discussion as to how this magazine, which must be bomb-proof, should be constructed.   At last a happy thought struck me.   I proposed that a tunnel should be made through the rear wall of the fort into the snow-bank outside; that into this should be inserted longitudinally an empty hogshead lying in the lumber-yard.   The snow should then be beaten down upon the hogshead and hardened by repeated freezings of water sprinkled upon it at night, the hogshead to be then withdrawn, and the circular aperture thus left shaped into an arched apartment by squaring down the side walls.

This plan was carried out so far as inserting the hogshead and beating down the snow upon it, but an unfriendly thaw setting in, the structure caved in as the hogshead was withdrawn. Nothing daunted, however, we repeated the operation, and a cold snap coming on, the walls became so solid as to stand firm on the second withdrawal of the hogshead. Our magazine was soon well filled with ammunition, little Ned Thompson, as powder-monkey, spending much time in shaping and storing the snow-balls.

Meantime the construction of the walls had gone on bravely, the corners being strengthened by towers, on the summit of one of which proudly waved the banner of the Lancers.

"Tell you what!" said Capt. Hunter, as he stood gazing admiringly upon the completed work, "this is a fort not to be sneezed at. Now let the enemy come on, if they dare."

He little knew how near at hand was the attack.

Next day, while at dinner, I was startled by little Jenny Ross rushing into the house, with her hood falling off her head, her cheeks all aflame, and shouting, —

"Harry! Harry! The Hog-Towners, the Hogtowners! They are tearing down the fort!"

Dropping knife and fork, I rushed out of the house, and running through the passage into the lumber-yard, beheld a startling scene. The enemy were indeed there in full force, and busily engaged in demolishing the walls of our much-prized fortification. For a moment I stood paralyzed, then seized with fiery indignation, I shouted, —

"Come out of that, you cowards!"

The enemy now for the first time observed me, and my challenge brought a shower of our own snowballs down upon me. I retired in good order behind a corner of the shed, but kept up a desultory fire in return, accompanied with such threats as, —

"You'll catch it for this! You dare n't come when we are in the fort."

Meantime the Hog-Towners went on demolishing the fort, in great haste, evidently fearing that its absent garrison might come to the rescue before their work of destruction was accomplished. I peppered them as fast as I could, but being one against many, they paid but little attention to me. Presently I heard a voice shouting, —

"Give it to 'em, Harry!"

It came from Bill Truman, who, with his head thrust out of one of the many windows of the twine factory, was cheering me on to the conflict. The enemy's attention being thus drawn to this new ally of mine, a shower of balls was directed against him, one of which struck Bill fairly on the head and caused him to suddenly withdraw from the field of view.

I now advanced from behind the corner of the shed, and with a well-aimed ball struck the leader of the Hog-Towners full in the face. Enraged by this he leaped forward, shouting savagely, and was about to pounce upon me when another ball, from some unobserved hand in the rear, struck him in the back of the neck. Alarmed at this attack in the rear, he turned about and we both beheld little Ned Thompson, half buried in a heap of snow on the top of one of the highest piles of boards behind the fort. He had heard the noise of the conflict at his home down Cross Street, and wading through the snow across Chaddock's intervening garden, had climbed the pile nearest the fence, from the top of which he looked down upon the scene of combat as from a vantage-ground.

"Good for you, Ned!" I shouted. "Hit him again!"

Ned needed no urging, and being a good shot, his balls began to tell on the invaders, who, finding themselves attacked front and rear, began to think of beating a retreat. Their leader, however, determined to punish me before retiring, and therefore ordered an attack upon me in full force. On they came, pelting me with snow-balls as they advanced. Thinking discretion the better part of valor, in this particular instance, at least, I retired to the porch of our house and awaited their attack upon the steps.

At this moment a ball thrown by their leader struck me on the forehead and caused me to see stars for a moment. My adversary shouted in triumph as he saw me rubbing my head; but while his mouth was widely distended in exultant laughter, a ball from an unexpected quarter entered it and suddenly stopped his wind. He stood for a moment with his arms extended, his mouth full of snow, and his eyes sticking out of his head, as if he had been suddenly sent for and could n't go.

"That 'll stop your mouth!" shouted a voice I well knew, and turning, I beheld Tim Bunce in the gateway, dancing and grimacing, his splay foot keeping time to the bobbing of his fiery red head.

"Fire away, Harry!" said he, "I 'm coming!"

Just then the enemy found themselves attacked in the rear by Ned Thompson, while other members of the Lancers, having been hastily summoned by little Jenny, began to gather on their front. Ben Hunter, Joe Jameson, and Si Sumner came running one after the other, eager to wreak vengeance on the invaders. The battle grew warm for a time, and the Hog-Towners, finding themselves likely to be surrounded in their enemy's country, beat a retreat through the lumber-yard and into the street, retiring rapidly towards their own territory, but keeping up a scattering fire from their rear-guard as we followed them up.

The enemy having been beaten off, we repaired to the fort to learn how far they had succeeded in demolishing it.   What a scene of ruin met our gaze! The walls were thrown down to the foundation, the roof of the magazine was broken in, and all our ammunition was gone.   A council of war was hastily called, and it was determined to rebuild the fort forthwith.   It would never do to allow the envious Hog-Towners to exult in the thought that they had forever destroyed the stronghold of the Liberty-Streeters.

Accordingly we set at work with a will, and soon had the satisfaction of seeing the walls restored. While thus engaged a few days after the battle, Ned Thompson remarked, —

"Boys, little Jenny Ross is sick.   They say she caught cold running through the snow on the day the Hog-Towners came down, and now she's got a fever."

This was sad news to all of us.   Jenny was a general favorite.   She was a bright, active little girl, and had taken great interest in the building of our fort.   She used to come and look on as the walls

went up, encouraging us in our work by her admiring remarks. She was the first to discover the
attack of the Hog-Towners and to give the alarm.

"Tell you what, fellers," said Si Sumner, "Jenny
is a jolly girl, and if anything happens to her, I shall
hate the Hog-Towners worse than ever."

This was the universal sentiment, and as day by
day we heard that Jenny grew worse we became sad
and thoughtful. At a meeting of the Lancers held
in the stable office, Jenny's condition was seriously
discussed, and it was unanimously resolved that some
expression of our regard for her was due from the
company.

Accordingly a contribution was raised among the
members to buy a dozen oranges, and I was deputed
to present them to her in the name of the company.

"Get the best you can find, Harry," said Ben
Hunter, "Delande has got some big Havanas."

I took great pains in picking out the oranges to
get sound and ripe ones, and went with a sinking
heart to the door of Jenny's home. It was a humble
cottage, and I can see now the little dark room into
which I was admitted by Jenny's mother, a toil-worn,
sad-faced woman. Little Jenny lay in the bed,
moaning with pain. All the brightness had gone
out of her once sunny face, which was now distorted
with suffering. But as I spoke her name she recog-

nized me, the moaning ceased for an instant, a smile like a gleam of sunlight broke over her features, and then instantly faded again into a look of anguish. That look haunts me still. I have witnessed many painful scenes, but none lingers in my memory and comes to me in the quiet hours of meditation like the sweet smile of that dying child, breaking out in the midst of her anguish in recognition of her play-fellow, and recalling for an instant the happy hours we had spent together.

Jenny died that night. When it was whispered around, next morning, among the boys, there were many sorrowful faces. To most of us it was the first time that death had come so near. I could remember when my mother first told me that all must die. It seemed then an incredible thing. Now it had become a dreadful reality. As some of us sat in Bill Truman's cottage, that evening, we talked of death, and tried to bring it home to our-selves that we should see little Jenny no more. We resolved to attend her funeral, and we walked, two by two, in the rear of the little procession of mourn-ers that followed her remains to the graveyard at the foot of the hill.

8

CHAPTER VIII.

TAR-BUCKET NIGHT.

AMONG the peculiar institutions of Landsport was its manner of celebrating the birthday of George Washington, the father of his country. The origin of the custom is lost in the mists of antiquity. Perhaps some fisherman, landing with a full fare on the 22d of February, blew a joyous blast on his horn in honor of the day and his own good luck, and so set all the other horns a going; perhaps the tar-barrel suspended, during the War of 1812, from a tall signal spar on the summit of the hill, to be fired should the enemy approach the harbor, suggested the burning of tar-buckets and bonfires. However this may be, certain it is that the blowing of fish-horns and the burning of tar-buckets on Washington's birthday had long been a custom which no Landsport boy, with any patriotic spirit, could by any possibility think of foregoing. If in thus honoring the memory of our great patriot his love of noise and fun found high gratification, why, so much the better. There were, indeed, a few people in the town who considered the custom "more honored in the breach than the observance," but they were ancient persons, in whom the blood of youth had long since cooled, and who, moreover, were suspected of a Tory-ish lack of reverence for the hero in whose honor it was observed.

As the eventful day approached every boy took pains to provide himself with a long tin horn, the manufacture of which was no small item of business in the tinners' shops. His next care was to procure and secrete in the cellar or barn a bucket or tub filled with tar and other combustible materials. This it was not so easy to obtain. The ship-yards and the marine railway, where the repairing of vessels went on, furnished most of the tar, and I am afraid were subjected to many predatory raids by the baser sort of boys. We Liberty Streeters always got our tar honestly, when we could. The tar-bucket having been secured, it was placed on a hand-sled and set on fire, to be drawn in triumphal procession through the town.

On the morning of the 22d of February every boy sallied forth with his horn, and the streets re-sounded with discordant blasts. This uproar con-tinued during the day, and as nightfall approached the tar-buckets were drawn forth, a long string of boys manning the rope and blowing horns as they marched along in the light of the blazing pitch At central points bonfires were lighted, around which gathered admiring crowds of spectators.

The biggest of these bonfires was always to be found at Gorham's Corner. This was an unsavory locality of the town, in bad repute because of the turbulent character of its inhabitants ; the centre of sailor boarding-houses, and the scene of street brawls and drunken rows. Now if the Hog-Towners were barbarians who swooped down upon us from the north, the Gorham's Corner boys were pirates who came up from the sea and despoiled us. The former were distant marauders from whom only an occasional incursion was to be feared ; the latter were the enemy at our gates, Gorham's Corner lying only a short distance away, at the foot of Centre Street. Between the two we Liberty-Streeters were trained to eternal vigilance.

The leader of the Gorham's Corner boys, in my time, was Dandy George, a big, rollicking, dashing buccaneer, who was greatly admired by his followers, and as cordially detested by us.

Our fort having been rebuilt, — to which, by the way, we now gave the name of Fort Defiance, in allusion to the futile attempt of the Hog-Towners to destroy it, — it was resolved to celebrate the approaching birthday of Washington with more than usual brilliancy. The matter of way and means was discussed at frequent conferences. Joe Jameson had a big hand-sled which he was willing to sacrifice in the cause of his country, for, truth to tell, the sled was usually consumed, with the tar-bucket placed upon it. A large supply of horns was obtained with pocket-money saved for the purpose. But whence was the tar-bucket to come? Jim Norton, who lived at the lower end of the town, and was only a Liberty-Streeter by adoption, being a crony of mine, solved the problem by saying, —

"Capt. McLellan had his brig in Sturdivant's dock last fall, to have her bottom graved, and the men left a half-barrel with lots of tar in the bottom, and I know where it is!"

"Can you get it?" said I.

"I guess I can, if Tom Turner has n't found it. He 's rummaging everywhere for tar-buckets for his big bonfire. The half-barrel is in the old shed on the wharf, and Dan Reeves, who lives at the head of the wharf, will help me get it. His father is one of the calkers, and I know he 'd as lief we 'd have it as not."

Jim was accordingly appointed a committee to procure the tar-bucket, with the injunction to be spry about it, lest Tom Turner should get it. The rest of us agreed to procure as much combustible matter as possible with which to fill the half-barrel.

On the morning of the 22d we sallied forth with

our horns, Ben · Hunter being the first to sound a
trumpet call.   Such a tooting as we kept up all day
long !   Our discordant blasts brought responses
from every part of the town, and the memory of the
father of his country was never more highly honored.

As evening approached, preparations were made
on all sides for bonfires and the tar-bucket proces-
sions.   There was to be a big blaze in Market
Square, and the boys of every neighborhood were to
turn out with their tar-buckets.   As yet we had
heard nothing from Jim Norton, and we began to
fear that he might fail us.

"I 'll bet Tom Turner got that tar-bucket," said
Si Sumner, who was always disposed to look on the
dark side of things.

"Don't you believe it," said I, feeling bound to
stand up for my friend.   "Jim 's wide awake and
knows what he 's about."

"That may be," remarked Joe Jameson, "but I
know that Tom Turner is always on hand and nobody ever gets ahead of him."

"Wait and see," was my confident response.

Even as I spoke a loud halloo was heard from the
direction of Middle Street, and presently Jim appeared, with two or three recruits whom he had
enlisted in his neighborhood, dragging the tar-barrel
on a sled behind them.

"Good on your head, Jim!" we all shouted.

"Boys," responded Jim, slewing the sled into view, "this is a prize from the sea, and we liked to have drowned Tom Turner in getting it."

"How was that?"

"Why, just as we were hauling the tar-barrel out of the shed, Tom Turner came down and claimed it as his. I said it was n't, for Dan Reeves's father said I might have it. Tom said it did n't belong to Reeves, and the real owner had given it to him. He tried to take it away from us. We pushed him off. The wharf was slippery, and he slid to the edge and went overboard. I tell you we were scared enough, but when we got to the edge of the wharf, expecting to see Tom struggling in the water, there he was on a cake of ice, floating in the dock! The tide was up, and he did n't have far to fall, so he was n't hurt, but his fall had pushed the ice out from the wharf, and he was sailing away to the other side of the dock. 'A pleasant voyage to you!' said I, but as we were in a hurry, we could n't stop to see him arrive safe in port."

We all laughed at Tom's involuntary voyage, and at once set about preparing for our parade. Ned Thompson came running in at the last moment.

"What made you so late, Ned?"

"Mother made me stop to change my clothes.

She said she was n't going to have me coming home with my best jacket all over tar."

"Why, Ned, you 've outgrown yourself," said Ben Hunter, with a quizzical look at Ned's arms and legs protruding through a cast-off suit.

Most of us had taken the precaution to put on our old caps and jackets, knowing by experience that those who touch pitch are sure to be defiled.

"Come, hurry, boys," cried Joe Jameson, "it 's time we were starting."

Si Sumner and I had been appointed firemen, our duty being to walk by the side of the sled and poke the fire, occasionally adding new fuel to it, while the rest. of the company manned the rope, each armed with his long tin horn, and vigorously blowing it from time to time as breath held out.

Such a grand spectacle as we made marching up the street, with a bobtail of the smaller fry following us! The blazing tar, the volume of thick black smoke rolling up from it, the tooting of the horns, and the loud word of command from Ben Hunter, with frequent hurrahs at the street-corners ; the meeting with other tar-bucket companies, the exchanging of salutes, and the bonfires blazing in the distance, all made up a stirring and highly patriotic scene.

We marched up Centre Street to Market Square,

then around the bonfire in the square, exchanging
cheers with the crowd surrounding it; then down
Congress Street, through Temple to Middle Street.
As we were passing the head of Union Street we
suddenly heard a loud voice crying, —

"Go for 'em, my hearties!"

Immediately a crowd of young ruffians rushed out
of the shadow at the corner of Union and Middle
Streets, where they had been lying in wait, and
attacked us with a volley of snow-balls. We knew
them at once for the Gorham's Corner boys. It was
their custom to roam about the streets and capture
tar-buckets to be added to their bonfire at the
corner.

Dandy George was at their head, and he made a
rush for the rope, followed by all his band of marauders. A hand-to-hand conflict ensued, in which Ben
Hunter grappled with Dandy, and in the struggle
both came near falling into the blazing tar-bucket.
As it was, Ben's head hit the sled as he fell, and
while we rushed to his rescue, tumbling pell-mell
over each other, the Gorham's Corner gang seized
the sled and ran off with it. Ben's head was bleeding as he rose, but he declared he was not much
hurt, and he was eager to pursue the enemy. While
we were debating the best course to take, a crowd of
boys was seen approaching up Middle Street. At

first we took them for another gang of the Gorham's Corner marauders, and prepared to stand on the defensive, but Jim Norton cried out, —

"It's the Down-Towners! I see Dan Reeves at their head."

As they came on Jim inquired, —

"Where's your tar-bucket, Dan?"

"The Gorham's Corner pirates have stolen it," was the doleful response.

"And ours, too," we replied.

Here was a situation! Two despoiled parties, each eager for revenge.

"Dan," said Ben, "let's join our forces and make a raid on them pirates. We can put out their bon-fire and give 'em a thrashing."

"Enough said!" replied Dan, and every boy expressed his eagerness to be led to the attack.

"Wait a moment," said Joe Jameson, who always had a prudent eye to ways and means, "let's plan a little; we'd better not all go together, but divide and attack them on two sides. Besides, we want some-thing with which to rake out their bonfire."

"Garden rakes!" said Ned Thompson; "we've got two at home."

"Good," replied Ben Hunter. "You run and get them, Ned, and the rest of you get some long poles, — clothes-poles will do. And, Harry, while we are getting things together, you run down Centre Street, and see how many of them there are at the bonfire, and which will be the best way to go at 'em."

Nothing loath, away I went toward the scene of the enemy's triumph. As I approached the foot of Centre Street I kept within the shade of the buildings, and getting behind a flight of stairs, watched the scene before me.

Gorham's Corner lay at the meeting of five ways. Centre Street ran down to it from Market Square. Fore Street entered it on one side, and Pleasant, Danforth, and York Streets on the other, while several narrow alleys led from near it down to the shore. These alleys were the haunts whence issued the ragged recruits of the pirate gang of the corner.

In the centre of the irregular area thus formed blazed the big bonfire, which was fed with the prizes captured by the marauding gangs sent out from this stronghold of the common enemy. Around it was a yelling and dancing crowd, in which men, women, and children mingled with the boys, who were the heroes of the hour. To my excited imagination they looked like demons, as they leaped about in the weird light of the bonfire.

While I was looking on, Dandy George and his gang came in, and the cry, "Another prize!" went up from the crowd.

"Three cheers for Dandy George!" cried some admiring follower of that hero, in the crowd.

Thereupon Dandy mounted a half-barrel, and said with a magniloquent air, —

"I don't want any cheers, boys, but let's go for another prize!"

This was greeted with loud cheers, and Dandy and his gang set off down Fore Street.

Now is our time, thought I, and I immediately formed a plan of attack. The Down-Towers should proceed down Cross Street and approach through Fore Street, while our party should go up Liberty Street to South Street, and, coming down into Pleasant, be ready to attack the enemy on the side opposite to that on which the Down-Towers were to make the assault.

This plan was readily adopted by the leaders of both parties, with the additional suggestion, made by Dan Reeves, that his party should go armed with big lumps of snow to throw upon the bonfire, while we were then to come on with our rakes and poles and finish the work by scattering it abroad.

As our party entered Pleasant Street, we came near being discovered by Wild Madge, one of the Gorham's Corner girls, who had been left to run wild in the streets. She was passing down Pleasant Street on her way to the bonfire, when Ben Hunter caught sight of her and called a halt. We waited until she with her companions had gone on their way, shouting and singing as they went. Then creeping along in the shadow of the buildings, we drew near the scene of action just as a loud shout went up from the Down-Towners, who, having a shorter distance to go, were first on the ground.

Dandy George, having taken away in his marauding party the more active spirits of the corner, we anticipated an easy victory. The gang around the bonfire were indeed taken by surprise, but they stood their ground. The Down-Towners rushed in and threw their lumps of snow upon the bonfire, which by this time was burning low, but immediately found themselves engaged in a hand-to-hand conflict. While the enemy was thus occupied we went in with a hurrah, on the side opposite to that on which the conflict raged, and with our rakes and poles began scattering the fire into the street.

While thus busily engaged we heard a tumult of angry voices in our rear, and beheld Wild Madge coming to the rescue at the head of a motley crowd of men, women, and girls, whom she had rallied from the outlying regions of the corner. From below the Bank, from Tom-cat Alley, from Stetson's Lane, they poured, a raging mob, eager to wreak vengeance on the invaders. We faced about and met them with a shower of snow-balls, but on they came.

"Fire! boys, fire! Meet them with fire," cried
Ben Hunter, catching a brand on his rake and hurl-
ing it at the advancing crowd. His example was
immediately followed, so far as we were able to seize
the half-burned brands and fling them at the enemy.
These kept them at bay for a moment, but the men
of the party rushed in, and seizing Joe Jameson and
others, gave them a terrible cuffing.

By this time the bonfire was extinguished and
darkness had shut down upon the scene. In the
hurly-burly and tumult of the conflict it was hard to
distinguish friend from foe. The Down-Towners,
hard pressed by the enemy, had retreated a short
distance down Fore Street, thus drawing off the origi-
nal defenders of the bonfire and leaving us to deal
only with the rescuing party from the alleys.

We were getting rather the worst of it, when loud
shouts were heard in the distance. They came from
Dandy George and his gang advancing in triumph up
Fore Street with another prize. Missing the blaze
of their bonfire and hearing the noise of the conflict,
they suspected the cause and came on with loud
cries for vengeance.

Finding themselves thus placed between two
bodies of the enemy, the Down-Towners retreated up
Cotton Street, and their assailants, joining Dandy's
gang, led them on to the assault upon us. But by

this time we had drawn off up Pleasant Street, and in the darkness easily beat a safe retreat.

When we reached the stable-yard, from which we had set out in such bright array, we were a sadly dilapidated and crestfallen company.

"Boys," said Tim Bunce, "let's count up the killed and wounded. There's Ben Hunter, got a bloody head. Joe Jameson, ears are tingling yet, I reckon. Si Sumner has got one trousers leg left, but won't he catch it for that daub of tar on his jacket!"

"Shut up!" retorted Si; "your red head has turned black with the tar on it!"

"See how my hand is burned by that brand I threw at 'em," said Ned Thompson.

"Never mind, boys," cried Ben Hunter, "we've put out their bonfire, and that's glory enough for one night."

CHAPTER IX.

STUB—SHORTS.

EARLY one Saturday morning, not long after the battle of the bonfire, I was awakened by a most discordant noise partaking of the nature of a screech and a growl. Lying still awhile to listen, and thinking in my half-dreamy state that perhaps the " Grand Caravan " had arrived, with all its wild animals, I heard, mingling with the screeching and growling, loud cries of " Gee, Star," and " Haw, Buck." Then I knew that the ear-splitting noise was caused by the sleds of the board teams grinding over the frozen snow on their way from Saccarappa to the wharves.

Our town was a great lumber port in those days, shipping staves, heading, and boards to the West Indies in low-decked brigs, which brought back molasses, sugar, and tropical fruits. Molasses was the great staple of importation, much of it being converted into rum in our distilleries, while not a little went to sweeten the coffee and cakes of the country people. The loading of the lumber and the unloading of the molasses made lively times on the wharves, and they were favorite, though half-forbidden resorts of us boys on half-holidays. Grandmother had told me never to go near the wharves. I might get drowned. She had known a boy who had been drowned by falling through a hole in the ice while skating on the frozen surface of the harbor. Still I did not consider the prohibition absolute, and occasionally went down with Hay-bag Ross on his chipping expeditions; for, in addition to his gathering of fodder for "Sleepy Davy," Hay-bag was accustomed to put up the stub-shorts which fell under the adze of the stevedore in the preparation for stowage in the hold of the vessel. These stub-shorts made excellent kindling, and eked out the fuel in many a household.

The grinding noise of the sleds reminded me that I had promised Hay-bag to go down to the wharves with him that very day. Accordingly I joined him early in the afternoon, taking Si Sumner and Jim Norton along. Hay-bag had provided himself, for the bestowal of the stub-shorts, with a huge basket strapped to his back.

It was one of those bright, brisk winter days which are so exhilarating a feature of our New England climate. The sky was clear and deeply blue, the sunshine bright, and the air stimulating as a cor-

dial. It was so bracing and invigorating that we
fairly flew along, as if it had given us wings. A
light, dry snow had fallen the previous night, lodging on post-tops and the naked branches of the trees
along the walks and in the gardens; a southerly
breeze springing up blew this lightly lodged snow in
fleecy clouds about us; we toyed with it as we ran
along, revelling in the bright sunshine and the bracing air.

Our spirits were heightened by the lively scenes
around us as we approached the wharves. Trucks
loaded with hogsheads of molasses were straining up
the steep bank; the slow-moving ox-teams from
Saccarappa were going down; there was a busy
throng of merchants, ship-masters, sailors, and steve-
dores attending the discharging of cargoes and the
loading of vessels for Havana, Guadalupe, or Trin-
idad.

As we reached the head of Central Wharf, there
passed us a long line of red pungs, driven by tall
men in blue frocks, with red sashes about their
waists, who stood up on short tail-boards projecting
from the rear of the pungs, which were loaded with
cheese and round hogs. These were Vermonters,
who had come down through the Notch of the
White Mountains, from their homes, more than a
hundred miles distant, to exchange their products

for sugar, salt fish, rum, and molasses, with a side of sole-leather over all.

"Them's the Varmonters," said Hay-bag. "Do ye see them round red boxes in the pungs? They've got their grub in them; big doughnuts, I tell ye, and cheese!" And Hay-bag smacked his lips as if already tasting those luxuries.

"Hah!" replied Jim Norton, with great disgust. "I've tasted them doughnuts and there ain't no sweetening in 'em. But the cheese is good."

Arrived at the scene of operations, we found a stevedore on top of a high pile of boards, adze in hand, with which he was dexterously cutting off the short stub left on one end of each board in sawing the log. The stub having been removed on one side, he turned the board over with the projecting point on the back of the adze, and proceeded to make that side smooth also. This was necessary to the better stowage of the boards, which were then passed into the hold of the vessel, where the head stevedore superintended the stowage.

We found a crowd of boys, with baskets, already on the ground, and each stub-short that fell was eagerly seized. Hay-bag found the filling of his basket no speedy matter, but with our aid the task was at last accomplished.

"Now let's go and lob molasses," said Hay-bag.

Nothing loath, we proceeded to the opposite side of the wharf, where a brig recently arrived from Cardenas was discharging a cargo of molasses. As each hogshead was hoisted from the hold by the men at the winch, it was swung on to the wharf, where coopers were engaged in rehooping those hogsheads which had sprung aleak. A custom-house officer was taking account of each hogshead as it came up, while on the wharf the gaugers, with overalls drawn over their trousers, were measuring the contents of each, and scratching it down in hieroglyphics on the side of the cask.

In order to measure the molasses, it was necessary to knock out the bungs of the hogsheads, which was done by striking on each side of them with a wooden mallet. The molasses being new, and still working, it bubbled up in a thick froth through the bung-hole of the hogshead. This was our opportunity. With improvised spoons, made of bits of shingles, we proceeded to "lob" the luscious foam.

A crowd of boys and girls from Gorham's Corner were present, engaged in dipping the escaping molasses into tin pails for home use. One of the boys recognized me as having been present at the battle of the bonfire, and with an angry scowl cried out, "Here's a Liberty Streeter," at the same time flinging a quantity of the sweet foam in my face.

"You stop that!" shouted Jim Norton, bristling up to my assailant, while I busied myself in trying to get my eyes open.

"You had better get the tar out of your hair before you come down here," was the retort of the Gorham's-Cornerite, who remembered that on the night of the battle he had given Jim a whack over the head with a tarry stick. The other boys began to gather about us, but just as matters were assuming a warlike aspect, Hay-bag whispered, "Capt. Blake is coming!" and scampered off down the wharf.

The captain did immediately appear on the scene, and seizing Jim Norton with one hand and my assailant with the other, marched them into his office, near at hand. Capt. Blake was the owner of the cargo and had an eye to the loss of his molasses rather than to the keeping of the peace between the two belligerents.

We followed Hay-bag and awaited the result at a distance. Presently Jim came out of the office, looking rather crestfallen.

"What did he do to you, Jim?"

"He said that if he ever caught me here again he'd cut my legs off close up to my ears!"

This awful threat gave us a distaste for molasses, and we proceeded to the end of the wharf, where lay the brig "Trim," about to sail for Matanzas. The last of the stores were going on board, the first mate was on the quarter-deck giving his orders in a loud and peremptory voice, and the sailors were hoisting the sails and shouting, "Ay, ay, sir!"

Just then a cart drove down the wharf, in which was the keeper of a sailor boarding-house, and a sailor who, as Hay-bag remarked, was "slewed," which was the sea-going phrase for half intoxicated. At the last moment he had made some opposition to going on the voyage, and so was brought down in custody of his landlord, who, having got possession of the advance of his wages, was bound to see him on board. He refused to move from the cart, in which was also his chest, but the sailor landlord and the ship-owner took him by main force and hustled him on board, swearing as he went. Once on deck, however, he turned respectfully to the mate for orders, and went at work with a will.

The sails were hoisted, the lines cut off, and the brig moved slowly down the harbor. We watched her until she entered the ship channel and slowly faded from sight. She careened badly, as though her cargo were not well stowed. She was never seen or heard of again, having probably foundered, with all on board. I have often thought of that poor sailor so reluctant to go on what proved to be his last voyage.

As we lingered on the wharf, viewing the busy scenes around us, Si Sumner spied a barrel in a corner, with the bung temptingly open. Thrusting his bit of shingle into it, he took a long lob, but immediately began to spit and sputter, jumping about and grimacing horribly.

" What 's the matter, Si ? " cried Jim.

" Fish-oil ! " replied poor Si, still spitting and sputtering.

" Did n't it taste good ? "

" You 'd better try it ! "

We were quite willing to let Si do all the tasting in that direction.

At the head of the wharf lay an old brig, partly dismantled. We went on board of her and began running about the deck.

" I 'll bet you can't touch the truck," said Jim Norton. Now I had always a disposition to climb, and it had long been my ambition to " touch the truck," as we called reaching the block at the masthead, through which were reeved the halyards by which the ship's flag was hoisted. It was considered a great achievement, and there was a tradition among the boys that Bill Truman had once not only touched the truck, but had actually thrown himself over upon it, lying on his stomach and extending his legs clear from the mast.

I was quite ready to accept Jim's challenge, and immediately began ascending the ratlines of the mainmast.

"I would n't go through the lubber-hole," said Jim, sarcastically.

"Never you fear," said I, as I grappled with the catharpings by which the maintop was reached. Going over the catharpings was not an easy thing to do, as it compelled an outward incline in order to get over the edge of the maintop. Most boys preferred crawling through the lubber-hole, though by so doing they were subjected to much ridicule from the more adventurous climbers.

From the maintop I went up to the cross-trees at the head of the topgallant-mast. From this point it was necessary to shin to the mast-head by the shrouds, and here came the difficult part of the undertaking. Unless a boy had a steady head and a good grip he was very apt to give up the task at this point. I braced myself for the effort, and shinned slowly up the shrouds, hand over hand, and with knees closely hugging the rope. Half-way up my strength nearly failed, and a downward glance made my head swim a little. Remembering an old sailor's advice to look aloft always, I cast my eyes upward, and, making one vigorous effort, hitched myself along, and was soon able to reach up and touch the truck.

A hurrah went up from my friends on deck, and I was glad to slide down the shroud and reach the maintop, where I paused to take breath. Here I met Jim Norton, who said, —

"You did well, Harry. You know Steve Miles? Well, he came down on the wharf once with a lot of fellers, and as he was climbing the rigging he fell and broke his arm, and all the fellers were so scared they ran away and left him. If it had n't been that somebody going up the wharf heard him crying, he would have had to stay there all night."

We remained on board some time, playing about the deck and hauling at the rigging. The throat halyards of the mainsail had rotted off at the boom, and hung loose and dangling. Si Sumner caught hold of the other end and hoisted it up. Thinking we ought to leave things as we found them, I went up the ratlines to reach the halyard and haul it down. While in this position I was seen from the office window of the owners of the brig, who immediately jumped to the conclusion that we were stealing the rigging to sell for old junk. Out ran one of them, while the other stood at the door and shouted, —

"Give 'em a good thrashing!"

Seeing danger ahead, Si and Jim tumbled out on to the wharf just in time to be caught by the irate ship-owner, who gave them both a sound cuffing about the ears.

Meantime I swung down upon the deck, ran to the opposite side of the brig, where I had seen a calker's raft lying in the dock and jumped down upon it. From the raft I saw a cake of ice floating in the dock, upon which I thought to escape to the opposite wharf. It was just beyond my reach, but getting down upon my knees, and placing one hand on a rim of ice adhering to the edge of the raft, I reached out with the other toward the floating ice. At that moment the rim of ice on which my hand rested gave way, and over I went, turning a complete summersault, and bringing up on the mud at the bottom of the dock, in about four feet of water. I scrambled on to my feet, and getting my head above water, cried lustily for help.

The ship-owner having come on board in search of me, looked over the rail, and seeing me rise dripping out of the icy brine, cried out, —

"Oh, you are there, are you? Served you right."

"Help me out," said I, pitifully, clinging to the edge of the raft, on to which I was unable to climb because of the crumbling ice along its edge. He came down on to the raft very leisurely, and taking a cool survey of my situation, instead of helping me out, told me to pick up my cap, which was floating near. Then he gave me a hand and pulled me on to the raft.

"Well," said he, surveying my dripping garments, "this will teach you not to come down on to the wharf stealing rigging"

"I was n't stealing," cried I, indignantly.

"Don't tell me that," was the reply.

It was in vain that I protested my innocence. I was told to depart, with the injunction never to be seen there again. I went on my way, burning with a sense of injustice that made me quite oblivious of my drenched condition. At the head of the wharf I met Ben Hunter.

"Why, Harry," said he, "you look like a drowned rat."

"I'm not drowned, but I wish old Harris was." And I told Ben the whole story.

"Well," said he, "what with the molasses on your face and your dip in the brine, you are in a sweet pickle. What will your grandmother say?"

"Help me out, Ben, won't you?'

"Yes, I will. You come home with me, and wash your face and dry your clothes, and she need never know anything about it."

A friend in need is a friend indeed. Ben's mother took me in hand, and I was put in so presentable a condition that I went home with a light heart.

CHAPTER X.

ON THE ICE.

THERE had been a "cold snap." For three nights in succession the mercury had fallen below zero. As I lay in my attic chamber I could hear the nails snap in the roof, — the small artillery of the frost, — and on awaking in the morning their glistening heads looked down upon me like stars. Oh, the getting out of bed on those cold mornings before the days of furnaces and steam! It was only repeated calls from the foot of the stairs that impelled me to fling off the blankets in a spirit of desperation, and make a dive for my clothes.

"Twenty degrees below zero," were the words I caught one morning on coming down to breakfast. "At this rate the harbor will be frozen over," said my uncle Tom, who, as a sea-faring man, naturally had an eye to the weather.

Sure enough, on my way to school I overtook Tim Bunce, who said, —

"Harry, the harbor froze over last night and we 're going a skating this afternoon. Can't you go with us ?"

This was a hard question to answer. I knew my grandmother's horror of the ice, but then she was absent from home, having gone on a visit into the country. I counted on persuading my aunt to permit me to go, and not caring to let Tim know that I might be prevented by home control, I told him quite confidently that I would be on hand at the appointed time.

It was not so easy as I had thought to persuade my aunt, but after much entreaty a qualified permission was given, with many injunctions to keep away from the dangerous places and to be home early.

"Remember, Harry," she said, "I don't know what I could say to your grandmother if anything happened to you while she is absent."

These words came back to me very vividly at a later period in the day.

As we approached the narbor the scene that met our gaze was very different from that presented to us on the day of our adventures on the wharves. It gave us the other side of winter. There were very few persons stirring in the streets. Traffic had been suspended by the extreme cold and the superabundance of snow. The Vermonters could n't get through the Notch, and were snowed up on the other side of the mountains. There was nothing doing on the wharves. A few coasters that had taken refuge in the harbor were caught in the ice. The sky was gray and leaden, and the surface of the harbor, instead of waves sparkling in the sunshine, presented a broad expanse of clear white ice and snow. It was, however, the scene of the only activity visible. Parties were crossing from the wharves to the shore of the cape opposite. Boys were dragging sleds over the ice, while skaters were skimming along its surface in large numbers. It gave me a strange sensation to be walking where I had never before seen anything but blue water. Many crossed over to the cape merely for the sake of saying they had accomplished that feat. It was a thing of which to tell in after years. It was in something of this spirit that, after skating far down the harbor, Jim Norton said,—

"Let's go down to Hog Island; we're almost there now."

It did indeed seem not far away, but distances on the ice, as on the water, are deceptive.

"Come on!" cried Tim Bunce, making a gyration that brought him down flat on his back and caused him to see stars in the leaden sky overhead.

"We don't propose to go that way," said Jim; "we might touch bottom."

Remembering my aunt's injunction, I made a feeble remonstrance, but was all too easily persuaded to go on with the rest. The island seemed so near.

As we got farther down the harbor, off the ship channel, the ice grew rough and hummucky. At intervals there were great cracks in it, which, however, we easily crossed. As we proceeded still farther from the shore the scene around us began to take on a strange, desolate aspect. The way became difficult and tiresome. Skates had long since been discarded as useless. We rambled on for a while, not without some enjoyment of the novelty of the situation, heightened perhaps by a sense of danger. At last Si Sumner's heart began to fail him.

"Look here, boys," said he, "I believe we have gone far enough. It will soon be getting dark."

"Don't back out now," shouted Jim, far in advance, "it is only a little farther."

We struggled on for some time longer, but as the ice grew more and more rough, with great gaping cracks, and the dull gray sky seemed shutting down upon us, Si again remonstrated, and we came to a halt. Looking around us, we were startled to find that we had somehow lost our bearings. In the gathering gloom the familiar shores had taken on new and strange aspects. And then they seemed so far away. Around us spread the desolate waste of ice, presenting a broad barrier between us and our homes. Our hearts sank as we took in the situation.

"I'm going back!" cried Si Sumner.

"And I'll go with you," said Tim, who for once forgot to put on a comical look.

"But which way will you go?" asked Jim, not without some visible concern.

For my part, I could n't answer the question. The scene had grown strange and terrible to me. I felt that we were lost on the ice. Si swept his eye around the fast-narrowing horizon, and pointing at a dimly looming outline in the distance, said, —

"I believe that is the city."

"No," replied Jim, "we did n't come that way. We ought to bear off more to the left. Don't you see that light?"

"That is on the cape," said Si. "I'm going the other way."

"Do as you please," replied Jim, who was not without a spice of self-will on occasion, "and see who will get home first."

He said this quite bravely, but I knew there was a doubt in his mind.

"Come, Harry," he continued, "let's be off. There's no time to be lost here."

Very reluctantly I followed Jim, while Si and Tim disappeared in the opposite direction. They seemed to me to take with them what little hope there was left to us. I called after them, but got no answer. Night seemed to shut down upon us all at once and swallow them up. Jim tried to keep up a good heart and declared that we should reach the city first. In my own mind there arose a vision of home, of the cosey fireside, the waiting supper, and my aunt growing anxious at my long absence.

"Jim," said I, with a great sinking at my heart, "are you sure this is the right way?"

"No, Harry, I ain't, but I'm pretty certain the other way isn't right, either. The fact is, we're lost."

He said this with a quaver in his voice that did not tend to encourage me. However, I felt it incumbent upon me to do my share towards keeping a stiff upper lip, so I said, —

"Well, we can't fail to strike the shore somewhere."

But as we struggled on in the increasing darkness, at times falling over the icy hummocks, which began to present the appearance of frozen waves, our desperate situation began to tell upon us with overpowering force.

"Harry," said Jim, "I'm sorry I asked you to come with me." And there were tears in his voice.

"Never mind, Jim, we'll keep together, whatever happens."

He took my hand and we stumbled on side by side. We had now lost all sense of the direction in which

10

we were going, and felt that we were aimlessly wandering, we knew not where. Fatigue and cold and hunger began to tell upon us, and we no longer had a word of cheer to offer to each other. How far away seemed home and friends and parents! How appalling was the desolate waste around us! Bitterly did I lament my folly in disobeying my aunt. Jim's thoughts, I knew, were like my own, and presently he said, —

"Harry, if you get home, tell my father — "

"Don't," sobbed I.

Not another word was said. We could not trust ourselves to speak, but still struggled slowly on, unable to direct our steps in the darkness which had now shut down. It seemed to me like the night of death. The world and all its brightness had gone far from me. My heart was full of pity for myself and of a great, dark fear. How terrible is death to the young, — death alone, in the darkness of night, far away from home and friends, while the soul cries, lost! lost! I could no longer control myself. I cried aloud, —

"O Jim!"

At that moment he sank from my sight into a great gap in the ice. I stood aghast as I saw him clutching at the edge of the ice, which crumbled beneath his hold.

In an instant a quick thought came to my mind. All this time I had been dragging my sled behind me. Again and again, owing to the roughness of the ice, I had been tempted to abandon it. But it was a present to me from a kind uncle, and I could not bear the thought of leaving it on the ice to float far out to sea. Now I was glad I had kept my hold upon it. I dared not venture near the hole into which Jim had fallen. Indeed, in the darkness, I would not well direct my steps, but I heard him utter an agonizing cry, —

"Harry!"

It was an appeal for help that could not be disregarded. Throwing myself flat on the ice, as far forward as I dared, I thrust the sled towards him and held on to the rope. Still clinging to the edge of the ice, he made a desperate reach, but lost his hold and disappeared below the surface. I uttered a cry of terror and drew myself forward. In an instant Jim's head reappeared, and he said, gaspingly, but in a hopeful tone, —

"I 've — touched — bottom!"

I thrust the sled towards him, he seized the bar, and with a long pull and a strong pull I drew him on to the ice. But, oh, how he shivered, and his teeth chattered, as he said, —

"I touched bottom, Harry. We can't be far from shore. Hurry! quick! or I shall freeze!'"

I seized him by the arm, and making a short circuit we crossed the gap in the shore ice, and soon saw looming before us a high bank. What joy to be on land again! The steep icy bank was not easily climbed, especially by Jim, encumbered as he was by wet and icy garments. I pulled him up to the top, however, where we found ourselves in a wood. We pushed on through this for some time, as fast as we would, and at last emerged into an open field. As we entered this I caught sight of a twinkling light in the distance, which, however, instantly disappeared. My heart bounded with joy, but sank again with disappointment as the light went out.

I felt certain, however, that I could follow the direction of the light, and we strugged slowly on through the deep snow.

"Are you sure you saw a light?" said Jim, who was growing weak and faint-hearted.

"Yes, I saw it plainly."

"Maybe it was only a jack-a-lantern."

"No," said I, assuming a confidence I did not wholly feel, "it came from a house, and we shall find it yet."

Still we stumbled on in the darkness, until Jim declared he could go no farther. At that moment, being in advance, I struck against some obstacle in the way. It was a fence! We joyfully clambered over it, feeling assured a house could not be far off. In fact, we had advanced but a few steps when I ran head-foremost against a door. I knew it was a door because the latch made itself painfully apparent to my head. I cried joyfully, —

"Here we are, Jim!" and pounded on the door with all my strength, at the same time crying loudly for help.

Presently a gruff voice asked, —

" Who 's there ? "

" Two lost boys."

The door was immediately opened, and we fairly tumbled into the entry. Some one seized us both and dragged us into a room. By this time a woman, half dressed, appeared with a light.

"Sakes alive!" said she, "who be ye?"

"Where d' ye come from at this time o' night?" said the man who admitted us, a grizzly old fisherman.

"Off the ice," said I.

"And what were ye a doin' on the ice?"

"We got lost, and Jim fell into a hole."

"Lord a massy!" said the woman, "don't ye see the boys is half froze? Don't stand there a jawing 'em. Rake open the fire and clap on some wood. They must have something hot."

With this the motherly old woman busied herself

in helping Jim strip off his wet and half-frozen garments, and soon had him wrapped in comfortable blankets, sitting before a blazing fire, kindled by the old man.

"Now," said the latter, "tell us who ye be"

We gave our names, with a history of our adventures, and asked, —

"Where are we?"

"Ye're in Zeb Stirling's house on Peak's Island, and it's mighty lucky for you ye're here. You'd no business to go wandering on the ice in sich weather as this. It's a wonder ye didn't freeze to death."

"Now, Zeb," said his wife, "don't ye go a scolding the boys. I'm proper glad we've got 'em here, safe and sound. But how on airth did ye find the house in sich a dark night?"

"We saw a light, but it disappeared as soon as we saw it."

"Wall," said the old man, "it's lucky ye saw it jest as ye did, for we was jest going to bed, and had put out the light, an' if ye'd ben half a minit later ye might hev made *your* bed in the snow."

"It's a rale Providence, if ever there was one," said the old lady, as she handed Jim a steaming bowl of hot tea, and busied herself spreading large slices of bread and butter, which we were not slow in devouring. After we were thoroughly dried and warmed, the old lady said, —

"It's time ye was a gitting to bed, for ye must be awful tired. You'll hev to sleep in the attic, for my son's darter is a sleeping in the spare room to-night. I wonder the gal has n't been out here afore this, arter all the racket. She's ginerally wide awake when anything's going on, 'cept in the morning, when it's time to git up, and then she's ekil, I tell her, to one o' the seven sleepers."

As we were preparing to mount the primitive open staircase that led to the loft I saw a round, rosy face, peering with a half-wondering, half-quizzical expression through a door held slightly ajar, in the rear of the room. Jim caught sight of the face at the same moment, and feeling that, wrapped as he was in his blankets, — his clothes having been hung by the fire to dry, — he did not make a very presentable figure, he hastened to get in front of me, that I might cover his retreat to the regions above.

"Do you suppose she saw me, Harry?"

"Well, she looked as if she saw something funny!"

"Tell you what, Harry, you'll have to go down in the morning and get my clothes for me."

"All right," said I, adding, as I cast a look around, "is n't this a jolly old place?"

We were in a small chamber under the roof, the side walls sloping down to the floor. In one corner was an old spinning-wheel, in another an ancient chest of drawers, while on the end wall hung bunches of dried herbs and strings of Indian corn.

"Yes," replied Jim, "as the old man says, we're lucky to be here, but what are they thinking about us at home?"

This gave us both some anxious thoughts, but as we lay awake for a while, we began rather to enjoy the novelty of the situation. It was so jolly to be so far away from home, amid such new and strange surroundings, and, withal, to find ourselves so cosey after our perilous adventures.

"Harry," said Jim, "this is equal to being ship-wrecked and cast ashore on a desolate island."

"A good deal better," I replied, nestling down in the blankets. "I wouldn't care to make my bed in the snow to-night."

"We came plaguy near it. But won't this be an adventure to tell the boys!"

With this comforting reflection we both fell fast asleep.

Some time towards morning we were awakened by the howling of the wind and the rocking of the house. A storm had arisen in the night, and the wind whistled and shrieked around the corner of the house like a mad thing. At times it would lull away, and then come back with a scream that made us cuddle close to each other. Then would come a hollow roar in the chimney and a blast that shook the house again. It seemed as if all the demons of the air were circling about us and seeking to demolish our shelter. The old house shivered and groaned like a living thing. As we lay and listened to the tumult of the elements, our thoughts went out upon the ice, and Jim whispered, in an awestruck tone, —

"Harry, do you s'pose Si and Tim got home safe?"

"O Jim, I cannot bear to think they are on the ice now! They went the other way, and that would carry them towards the city."

We lay awake for a long time listening to the voices of the gale, almost fearing at times that it would sweep away the house and all in it. When at last the morning dawned, we found ridges of snow on the bed that had sifted in through the cracks in the roof. The storm still continued to rage, and we lay a long time listening to its hollow roar, with anxious thoughts of home and how we were to get there.

"Wall, boys," said the fisherman, as we appeared in the room below, "it's lucky ye got here jest as ye did. This nor'easter has broke up the ice, and it's

going out of the harbor. Ye'll hev to stay here to-
day."

This was unwelcome news. Knowing how anxious our friends would be concerning our safety,
we had hoped to get home that day.

"I should think the ice might have held out one
day longer," said Jim.

"Speak well o' the bridge that carried ye safe
over, my lad," said Stirling. "If it had n't ben fer
the ice ye'd never ha' ben here by this warm fire,
and ye'd never seen my granddarter, either. This
is Susie."

The young girl thus introduced came frankly forward and said, —

"I'm so glad you found our house before the
storm came. You must have suffered terribly."

We both very bravely protested that we did n't
mind the cold, but were fain to admit that we were
glad we were sheltered when the storm came on.
Miss Susie busied herself in setting the table for
breakfast, and presently her grandmother bustled in
with a steaming dish of chowder.

"I thought I'd hev somethin' hot for ye this cold
mornin'. I hope ye slep' well las' night. Ye must
ha' ben proper tired. But, sakes alive! I could n't
sleep a wink. Sich a howlin' an' a screechin' as the
wind kept up, I never did hear in all my born days."

"Oh, yes, ye hev, marm," said the old man. "Don't ye remember that heavy nor'easter that blowed the barn down ten years ago?"

"Yes," said the old lady, in a saddened tone, "that was when the "Hero" was wrecked on the back side o' the island, an' only one man was saved."

"An' a narrer chance he hed, too," continued the fisherman; "I never see the beat on 't. There was twelve on 'em aboard, and all on 'em was drownded but him. He was down in the hol' when she went to pieces, and he said he thought his time was come. But he grabbed hol' of a barrel and held on for dear life, and was jest washed ashore with it. But come, boys, this 'ere chowder won't wait for no long yarns."

After breakfast we went out to take a look at the ice. As Stirling had said, it was broken up by the violence of the gale, and in the lower bay great fragments were tossing and heaving, and grinding together, while towards the town we could see blue water and masses of ice drifting out to sea through the ship channel. It was plain there was no reaching our homes that day.

As the gale continued, we returned to the house, depressed with the thought of the anxious ones at home.

"I'm afraid they'll think we are drowned," said Jim.

"Now, boys," said Mrs. Stirling, "don't ye be down-hearted. This 'ere gale is a driving the ice right out to sea, and by to-morrow it'll be all clear water. Then father'll take ye home, — he's got to go to town any way to git some groceries, — and they'll be proper glad to see ye, I'll be bound. You set here in the forenoon, and Susie she'll come in, by and by, and chirk ye up."

We were glad of the company of Miss Susie, and at her solicitation related our adventures on the ice with all the modesty of heroes.

Susie expressed great sympathy with our sufferings, and on her part told how she once got adrift in her grandfather's boat, and was floating out to sea in a fog, when she was picked up by a fishing schooner entering the harbor.

As we sat conversing, I observed, hanging on the chimney above the great open fireplace, a very long fowling-piece, of ancient pattern.

"That's a very old gun, is n't it, Miss Susie," said I.

"Yes, grandfather sets great store by that gun. He shot off an Englisman's hand with it."

"How was that?" I cried eagerly, scenting a story in the distance.

"Oh, it was in the last war! I don't remember the rights of it. You must get grandfather to tell you how it was."

After supper, as we sat around the open fire of wood and listened to the storm still raging and shaking the loose window-frames, the old fisherman entered, wearing his weather-beaten sou'wester. He had been out doing his "chores," he said, and added, —

"This 'ere rain 'll finish the ice, boys, an' it will be all clear weather by mornin'. We'll go up to town fluking."

The falling snow had indeed turned to rain; we could hear it beating against the window-panes, and the sound added a sense of comfort to the cosiness of our situation.

As Stirling took his seat by the fire, I ventured to remark, by way of opening the door to the story of the gun, —

"That's a curious old fowling-piece you've got up there, Mr. Stirling."

"Yes, that 'ere gun was bought in Liverpool mor'n forty year ago. Cap'n Trefethen paid fourteen guineas for 't. It's a fowling-piece, and many's the old squaw * I've shot with it."

"It must be a very heavy piece," said Jim.

"Yes," replied the old man, reaching up and taking down the gun, "jest you heft it. That 'ere gun weighs twenty-seven pounds, and it's six feet an' a half long."

_____

* A species of wild duck.

We found it, indeed, difficult to hold it out at arm's length.

"I suppose," said I, "that it would send a ball a long distance."

"Yes, I 've knowed it to hit the mark a quarter of a mile off."

"Was that when you hit the Englishman's hand?"

"Oh, ho! Susie 's ben a telling ye about this, hes she?"

"Yes, sir, she said it was in the last war."

"Wall, I don't mind telling ye how 't was. But fust le' me put another log on the fire. There, that 'll last till bedtime."

And as he spoke the flame burst out and went crackling and dancing up the wide-mouthed chimney.

"But about that shooting the Englishman's hand off," continued Mr. Stirling, seating himself comfortably by the blazing fire. "Ye see in the last war the English cruisers used to be mighty sarsy out here in the bay, and chased and boarded us fishermen whenever they got a chance. One day — it was Independence Day — I was hoein' taters out in the field when I see Neighbor Clark, who went out fishing in the mornin', pulling fer the shore for dear life, with an English armed schooner behind him. So I said to the chap who was hoein' with me, 'Let 's git the guns and stand by him.' Pretty soon the

Englishman did n't dare come no furder on account of the rocks, so he lowered his boat, and eight men pulled away arter Clark. He was rale pluck, and held on like a good one. Soon they dropped their oars, and all hands fired slap into him. Somehow or other they did n't hit him, so we hurrahed and fired at them and they pulled off to the schooner again. The schooner, she kep' along shore till she got over there by the woods, an' then I was afeared they 'd come ashore and steal a critter. So we went over through the woods, an' there she lay, about a quarter of a mile from the shore. When they see us they fired a nine-pounder at us. I hed the big fowlin'-piece, an' so I crep' up to the bank and fired. She was a full quarter of a mile off, but I thought p'r'aps I might hit 'em. Arter I fired they did n't seem to like it, but fired their old cannon at us ag'in and then stood off an' we saw no more of 'em.

"I never should 'a' knowed what that shot did if it hed n't a bin there was some Yankee prisoners aboard. They landed 'em down to Harpswell, an' when they come back they told Cap'n Knights, that lived over to the ferry way, that that shot hit the cap'n o' the schooner right in the wrist, so that he had to have his hand cut off. He was standin' with his hand on the main shrouds, and the ball hit him right in the wrist. The Englishmen swore the Yankees hed a swivel ashore there."

"Did they never come ashore here during the war?"

"No, they took good care not to do that. But, boys, it's nigh bedtime. In the mornin' we'll see about gittin on ye home to your folks. I s'p'ose they're proper scared about ye."

On awaking next morning we found that it was as the old fisherman had said it would be, bright and clear. A northwest wind was blowing, and as we looked out of the little window in our attic chamber, we could see the blue waves dancing, where two days before all had been dull ice.

"Hurrah for home!" shouted Jim

We went down the stairs with a rush, and were soon out upon the shore. Mr. Stirling was preparing to launch his boat, but to our impatient inquiries replied that we must have some breakfast before starting.

We had scarcely thought of that, but were quite ready to do justice to the salt mackerel and johnny-cake set before us. Bidding Mrs. Stirling and Susie good by, with hearty thanks for their kindness, we left the house with many parting injunctions from the old lady to come and visit her the next summer.

While impatiently waiting for Mr. Stirling to get his boat in good trim, we chanced to spy another boat coming down the harbor. We thought nothing of it at first, but when we saw she was making for Hog Island, the thought struck me that she might be in search of us. I said as much to Mr. Stirling, and he told me to go up to the house and get his spy-glass, and we might be able to see who was on board of her. At first I could n't make them out, but presently one of the men turned towards us, and I plainly saw he was my uncle Tom.

I gave a shout and Jim, seizing the glass, soon cried out, —

" My father is there, too."

Thereupon we both shouted and waved our caps, and jumped up and down, until the old fisherman said, —

" Why, boys, they 'll think ye 're clean gone crazy. But shout away, an' you 'll fetch 'em."

Our cries did indeed attract the attention of the men in the boat, and presently we had the pleasure of seeing her come about and make for the spot where we stood. As she drew near I heard my uncle say, —

"Thank God, it is the boys!"

We were not long in leaping into the boat and rushing into their arms. The story of our escape was soon told, and Mr. Stirling, who stood by with a smiling face, was heartily thanked by my uncle and Jim's father. He refused all compensation, saying, —

11

"The boys are welcome, an' I hope they'll come down again, but not on the ice."

As we took our seats in the boat, my eyes fell on a familiar object lying on the bottom.

"My sled!" I cried.

"Yes," said my uncle. "We took that off a cake of ice as we came down. When we first saw it I did n't think of picking it up, but presently I recognized it as yours, and then I thought I should never see you again. But Mr. Norton said he thought you might have abandoned it while making for the land, so I plucked up heart again."

"But how did Si and Tim get home?"

"They had a pretty tough time of it, but landed back of the Neck, and got home safe before the storm set in. Si said he thought you must have landed on the cape, so we went there first, and, not hearing anything of you, were making for Hog Island when you hailed us."

I pass over the meeting with my aunt, who, it is needless to say, had been terribly alarmed at my long absence. As for my grandmother, both my uncle and aunt thought it best, on her return, not to tell her of my adventure for the present. When some time after she heard of it, she looked up over her glasses at me and said, —

"Harry!"

CHAPTER XI.

WE VISIT THE TROPICS AND ENGAGE IN A SEA-FIGHT.

ONE bright morning in June a party of us boys found ourselves once more on the wharves. After my experience on the ice I had no desire to visit them again during the winter, but now the scene was changed. The sun shone brightly, the air was soft and balmy, with a breath of spring in it that seemed to have been wafted from the Fortunate Isles, a light breeze rippled the surface of the water, and the harbor was all alive with craft spreading their sails in departure or arrival.

We had come down to witness the arrival of the brig "Beulah," Capt. Fox, whom Ben Hunter claimed as his uncle. She had been signalled at the Observatory, and the time-balls indicated that she was only an hour's sail outside.

We took our position at the end of Long Wharf, and kept our eyes fastened on the entrance to the harbor, a narrow passage running out to sea between the cape shore and Bangs's Island. Presently Ben Hunter cried out, —

" There she is ! "

The topmasts of a brig were seen rising above the land, and she soon came into view and sailed slowly up the harbor. She was deeply ladened, having not only a cargo of molasses in the hold, but two tiers of hogsheads on deck. As she drew near the wharf there were hailings and greetings between the captain and his friends, and Ben was not behind in his demonstrations of welcome, which were cordially recognized by his uncle on the quarter-deck.

The sailors were running up the rigging to furl the sails, and among them we recognized our old playmate, Bill Truman. Bill had left the twine factory for a sea-faring life some months before, and was now returning from his first voyage. We hailed him with delight, to which Bill, being still under ship's discipline, responded only by expressive gestures. Once on board, we gathered around him, and Jim Norton, who had cherished longings to be a sailor, which at time, found expression in his wearing a tarpaulin hat, and dipping his hands in coal-tar, in Dyer's ship-yard, to give them the real sailor grime, asked him, —

" How do you like being a sailor, Bill ? "

" It 's a dog's life ; but come down into the fo'castle and see how we live."

We went down the narrow companionway, into a

dark, dingy hole, the air in which was strongly im-
pregnated with a compound odor of tar, bilge-water,
and sour molasses.   When our eyes had become accustomed to the darkness, we dimly discerned a row
of bunks on each side of the narrow space, in front of
each of which was the chest of the sailor occupying it.

"Do you sleep in there?" asked Jim, in a tone of
disgust.

"Sartin, and we 're mighty glad to turn in after a
watch on deck, I can tell you."

"Do you eat here, too?"

"Of course we do.   You did n't s'pose we dined
with the cap'n, did you!   Or p'r'aps you thought we
had a dining-room set apart for us!" said Bill, with a
laugh.

"But where 's your table?"

"There," replied Bill, pointing to the floor.

"You don't sit on the floor to eat your meals!"

"Oh, no, of course not!   Don't you see the dining-
table, and the mahogany chairs all setting round?"
replied Bill, with a quizzical look.   Then he added,
"Yes, Jim, we do sit on the floor, and I 'll tell you
how it 's done.   One of us goes to the caboose and
gets the grub in a kid.   It 's mostly salt beef, and
mighty tough at that.   He sets it down here on the
floor, we all squat round it, and fall to with our jack-
knives."

"Does n't anybody say grace?" asked Ned Thompson, who was accustomed at home to all the proprieties of a Christian table.

"Say grace," replied Bill, with a grin. "Oh, yes, we say grace! P'r'aps you never heard a sailor's prayer over his meat. I'll repeat it to you. When we 're all sitting round the kid, one of us takes up the toughest piece of beef and says, —

'Old horse! old horse! what brought you here?'

Then another speaks up for the old horse, and says, —

> 'From Saccarap' to Portland Pier,
> I 've carted boards this many a year,
> Till, killed by blows and sore abuse,
> They salted me down for sailors' use.
> The sailors they do me despise,
> They turn me over, and damn my eyes,
> Cut off my meat, and scrape my bones,
> And pitch me over to Davy Jones.'

That 's the grace we say," concluded Bill.

"I should think you 'd say it with a very bad grace," remarked Jim Norton, whose visions of the delights of a sailor's life began to fade away before this matter-of-fact version of them.

"But do you really eat old horse?" asked Ned Thompson, in a tone of horror.

"They say we do. Anyhow, the best pieces are all

picked out for the cap'n's table. We don't get any fat, I can tell you."

"That's real mean," said Ned.

"But tell us about Havana," said Si Sumner; "did n't you see strange sights there?"

"I did n't see nothing!"

"Why, did n't you go ashore, and go out to the plantations, and see the oranges growing, and the niggers and things?"

"No! you don't get no chance to go ashore. You're just kept aboard, off in the harbor, all the time, working like a slave, discharging and taking in cargo."

This revelation of a sailor's life fell like a wet blanket on our aspirations for adventures and sight-seeing abroad.

"Well," said Ned Thompson, "I'd rather go to sea in John's way than Jack's way."

This was in allusion to a book we had been reading, which told about two boys who were determined to see the world, but set about it in different ways. John learned a trade, was industrious, laid up money, and then went abroad as a passenger, and saw many strange sights in foreign lands, while Jack went to sea as a common sailor, never rose to the quarter-deck, because he would not study navigation, and saw nothing of the foreign lands whose ports he visited. Some of us had been disposed to stick out stoutly for Jack's way and the charms of a sailor's life, in spite of this discouraging view of them, but there was no gainsaying Bill's account of his experience. Jim Norton looked very much down in the mouth.

"Cheer up," said Bill, clapping him on the shoulder ; "you can go to sea in John's way, if you're smart enough."

"Halloa, down there!" cried Ben Hunter, thrusting his head down the companionway. He had been with his uncle in the cabin, while we had been talking with Bill in the forecastle. "Come on deck and get some sugar-cane."

We all tumbled up as fast as possible, and found Ben with a tall stalk of the sugar plant, which he generously cut into lengths and divided among us. As we chewed the cane and sucked the saccharine juice, the gloom which the forecastle and its revelations of a sailor's hardships had thrown over us began to fade away, and a life on the ocean wave assumed something of its old attractiveness. Presently Capt. Fox called out, —

"Boys, here's a box of oranges partly decayed; you can pick them over and help yourselves."

Matters now began indeed to brighten! It was as good as being in the West Indies to sit there on the quarter-deck and suck sugar-cane and eat oranges fresh from Havana. John's way could n't be better than this. There was a tropical air in our surroundings that carried us far away from home. The shipping around us, the dash of the waves, the balmy atmosphere, the fragrance of the oranges, all conspired to transport us to distant lands far away over the blue ocean.

As we dipped into the box of oranges, we threw overboard those that were decayed. Presently an angry voice was heard, —

"Mind what you 're about aboard there!"

We looked over the rail, and there were Dandy George and two of his satellites going past in a row-boat. One of the decayed oranges had struck the boat. As Ben leaned over the rail, and was about to reply, Dandy splashed his oar in the water and threw a quantity of it in Ben's face. We all sprang to our feet, and Ben shouted, gaspingly, as he mopped his face, "Pelt 'em, boys, pelt 'em!"

How the rotten oranges did fly! Dandy stood stoutly up with his oar and splashed the water at us, but presently a big orange, very much decayed, took him fairly in the face, and he dropped into the boat as if he had been shot.

"The enemy has struck his colors," said Ben, but he did n't reckon on Dandy's pluck. That hero soon

recovered himself, and while hew ashed his face with
one hand, still splashed away with the other, at the
same time exhorting his comrades to stand up to the
fight.

Still the oranges flew, and Dandy and his companions were well bespattered, while we got an occasional drenching from their oars and the baling
dipper. As the fight grew hot we no longer stopped
to select decayed fruit, but pelted them with sound
oranges as well. The golden balls were more effective than the rotten ones. They proved a temptation
which the enemy could not withstand. They
attempted to catch them, and were thus thrown off
their guard. As one of them leaned back to catch
an orange, he lost his balance and fell overboard.
The boat drifted away from him, and he came up
alongside the brig.

Bill Truman, who had hastened aft at the sound of
the conflict, snatched up a boat-hook, and catching
the hook in the seat of his breeches just as he was
going down again, held him fast, while we ran to the
rescue and soon drew him on board, dripping and
squirming like a sea-green lobster fresh from the
brine.

His comrades, seeing his rescue, rowed away and
left him a prisoner in the hands of the enemy. He
was very disconsolate at first, and began to cry and

swear and threaten vengeance upon us : but we com-
forted him with oranges, and when Ned Thompson
added thereto a great chunk of sugar-cane, his wrath
was mollified, he shook himself and fairly beamed upon
us as he scrambled on shore and ran up the wharf.

A little sweetening goes a great way in conquering
an enemy.

CHAPTER XII.

A VOYAGE OF DISCOVERY.

On the morning succeeding our adventure on board the "Beulah" I met a number of the boys in the yard of the stage-coach stable. They were discussing the best way of spending the half-holiday of Saturday.

"I'll tell you what we'll do," said Ben Hunter. "My uncle will let us take his yawl boat and we'll go on a voyage of discovery down the bay."

"Agreed!" cried we all.

"And we'll take lines and catch some fish," said Si Sumner.

"And a pan to fry them in," added Tim Bunce.

"Yes, and some biscuit," continued Joe Jameson.

"And some cake," supplemented Ned Thompson, who knew where he could get it at home.

All matters being arranged, on the following morning we set out on our excursion down the bay. The yawl had no sail, and we could not have managed it if she had. We felt equal to the oars, however, and were soon gliding over the smooth waters of the harbor under the steady pull of Ben Hunter and Joe Jameson.

There was exhilaration in the thought that we were fairly afloat and on our way to regions new to us, for most of us had never before visited the islands. As we receded from the shore the city rose behind us on its elevated peninsula, its church spires rising above the long lines of trees that shaded its streets, while the observatory on the hill at its eastern extremity stood boldly out, a well-known landmark. The opposite shore of the cape sheltered the snug harbor from the sea, and where it ended the islands took up the sheltering line of land and continued it far down the bay, with the ship channel and out-reaching "sounds" between them, giving approach from the broad ocean beyond.

As we neared the ship channel, the principal entrance to the harbor, the fort on the cape came into view, and it was unanimously resolved to pay it a visit.

"We'll capture it, like the bold buccaneers," said Ben Hunter, who had been reading an account of Drake's voyages.

"The fort sogers will have something to say about that," replied Tim.

As we approached the wharf we saw a boy standing on the end of it, apparently watching our advance. He was dressed in uniform, and stood very straight and still.

"Halloa!" shouted Ben Hunter.

"Halloa!" replied the young soldier.

He was a very sober chap, and looked at us in a solemn sort of way.

"Can we go into the fort?"

"Yes."

Under the lead of our guide we went into the enclosure, crossed the parade-ground, where a squad of soldiers were going through the manual of arms, and entering a gateway in a brick wall, found ourselves in the fort. On the top of the sodded walls heavy guns were mounted, pointing down the ship channel.

"Do you s'pose a man-o'-war could get past this fort?" asked Ben Hunter.

"No!" replied our guide. "We'd blow her out of the water."

"Do you like being a soger?" asked Ned Thompson.

"Yes, I do. I never was anything else."

"Was you born a soger?" asked Ned, looking at him with admiring eyes.

"I was born in a fort. My father is an officer in the army of the United States," replied the soldier boy, with great dignity.

"Have you always lived here?"

"Oh, no! I've lived in a good many forts. A

soldier never knows to-day where he may be ordered to-morrow."

"Well," said Ned. " I 'd rather have a home."

" I 've had a good many homes," was the reply.

Looking across the ship channel, we saw another fort on an island, which also commanded the channel, and the passage out by •White Head, a bold promontory at the eastern end of Bangs's Island.

"That is Fort Scammell," said our guide. " My father says it is named for Gen. Scammell of the Revolutionary army.

"What 's that odd-looking building in it?" asked Joe Jameson.

" That 's a block-house."

"What 's it there for?"

"To defend the harbor from the enemy's ships."

"Are there any guns in it?"

" Yes."

"I thought," said Ben Hunter, "that block-houses were only used in old times for defence against the Indians."

"Let 's go and look at the old settler," said Joe ; and with a word of good-by to our stately young guide, we were soon on our way across the channel.

The old sergeant in charge of the fort admitted us, and we examined the block-house with much interest. It was built of pine and oak timbers, about fourteen

inches square, laid upon one another, and each one
well pinned and dowelled to the one below. The
building was octagon in form, two stories high, the
upper story projecting over the lower. In the upper
story, on four of the sides, were embrasures for four
cannon. In the floor of the projecting portion of
this story were a number of small openings.

"What are these holes in the floor?" asked Joe.

"They are for shooting down upon the enemy if
he should land and make an attempt to take the
fort," replied the sergeant.

"Yes, and to pour hot water down on 'em," said Si
Sumner. "I've heard my father tell about that.
The Indians used to try to set the block-house on
fire, and when they came near the walls they'd scald
'em."

"That was a long time ago," said the sergeant.

In the centre of the lower story was a magazine
built of bricks, and in the walls were loop-holes for
musketry. The block-house stood in an enclosure,
one side of which was guarded by a stone-wall with
fixtures for mounting six cannon, while on the other
side was a stockade formed of cedar posts about
eight feet high.

"This isn't much of a fort," said Ben. Yet it is a
fact that in those days our military authorities considered it capable of combating anything that might

be brought against it. Steel-clad ships had not then been thought of.

Returning to our boat, we pulled down Hog Island Roads, a beautiful passage between two islands, the one presenting a high green bank, the other a perpendicular wall of rock crowned with a dense forest growth.

"Peak's Island!" cried Jim Norton, "and there's Stirling's cottage."

We both waved our caps, and a young girl standing in the door, whom we felt must be Susie, responded with her handkerchief. Jim and I wanted to go ashore, but Ben was bound for Diamond Cove, on the opposite island and we were obliged to yield to his plans.

"We haven't time to land there now," said he; "we'll go there another time."

"Did you come all this way on the ice?" asked Ned Thompson, looking back toward the distant city. It did seem incredible that we had passed over that vast watery space on foot.

The day had grown very warm. The sun beat down fiercely, and we all, more especially those of us who had labored at the oars, began to suffer from thirst.

"Why didn't you bring a jug of water?" said Jim, who had been invited to join us at the last moment.

"We did n't think of it," replied Ben, "besides, when ships start on voyages of discovery they always get short of water and provisions."

Our thirst impelled us to renewed exertions at the oars, and after a long pull we rounded Bounty Head, at the eastern end of Hog Island, and soon made the entrance of Diamond Cove. This was a deep indentation in the shore of Hog Island, presenting a beautiful and secluded retreat, often visited by picnic parties from the city. Off against its entrance, sheltering it from the waves of the bay, lay a small, low island known as Cow Island. The two projecting arms of Hog Island enclosing the cove presented high rocky walls, surmounted with a tangle of trees and underbrush, while at the head of the cove a low grassy bank sloped down to the water's edge from the woods in the rear.

Entering the cove, we felt ourselves secluded in a little world of our own, and leaping on the beach took possession as if it were a newly discovered land. Our first thought was of water. After a long search I was fortunate enough to discover a little trickling stream at the foot of the wall of rock that enclosed the cove on the north, and digging in the sand brought to light a spring, which soon filled the cavity I had made.

After refreshing ourselves with draughts from this

fountain, it was resolved to proceed to the fishing ground near the shore of Cow Island. Here we had not long dropped our lines before I felt a nibble and drew in a lively mackerel. Tim Bunce pulled in another, and soon the sport grew fast and furious. We had struck a school of mackerel and for half an hour had rare sport in pulling them in.

By this time we began to think of supper, and returning to the cove took possession of one of the fireplaces built of stones which former visitors had left there. While some of us gathered fallen branches in the woods, Tim undertook to split and clean the mackerel. A fire was built, the frying-pan produced, and then Tim cried out, —

"Where's the pork?"

"Pork!" said Ben Hunter; "you don't want pork to cook mackerel."

A hot dispute ensued between Ben and Tim as to the proper way of cooking a mackerel, Tim insisting that his mother always fried them in pork fat, while Ben said they should be broiled. It ended in Tim's slapping a mackerel into the pan and placing it over the fire. The fire blazed, the mackerel sizzled, and we stood around in eager anticipation of the feast, for by this time we had grown ravenously hungry. But when the pan was taken from the fire the mackerel objected to leaving it, sticking fast to the bottom, and when fragments were torn off they were found to be not particularly palatable. Ned Thomp. son spit out a morsel in disgust.

"Now," said Ben, "let me broil one, and you'll see the difference."

He thereupon proceeded, in lack of a gridiron, to lay some sticks across the fire, on which he placed a mackerel. The sticks caught fire and broke and the mackerel fell upon the coals.

"Never mind," said Ben, "it'll brown all the better. A mackerel ought always to be well browned."

But the fire smoked, and the mackerel, when drawn from it by the tail, was not only browned but blackened to a degree that obscured its identity. Tim said it looked like a dirty dish-rag, a remark highly resented by Ben. It so disgusted Ned Thompson that he refused to touch a morsel of it. Ben, however, fell to and declared that all it wanted was a little salt, which Tim proposed he should supply by dipping it in the salt water at our feet.

We did n't greatly relish the feast, but managed to make a supper on biscuit and water, — real sailor fare, as Tim said.

In the long June day there were still some hours of daylight, and Ben proposed that before going home we should land on Cow Island and explore the old barn which stood upon it, with wide-open doors.

We found the barn empty, save for a little hay scattered over the floor, and soon wandered away from it to the farther end of the island, where we amused ourselves for some time in picking up shells on the shore. Presently Ned Thompson cried, —

" What 's that ? "

Looking in the direction in which he eagerly pointed we saw a round black head rising above the water. Soon another broke water near the first, and we could see that the creatures had large round eyes.

" They 're mermaids ! " said Ned Thompson, in an awe-struck tone.

" Ha ! ha ! " laughed Ben, " where are their looking-glasses ? "

" I 'll tell you what they are," said Joe Jameson. " They are seals. I 've heard my father tell about 'em. They breed on one of the little rocky islands in the bay." By this time they had disappeared beneath the water, and we watched in vain for their reappearance.

" Come," said Ben, " it 's time we started if we are going to get home before dark."

But on reaching the shore we found the boat high and dry on the flats. The tide had gone out during our absence, leaving a long expanse of mud over which the boat must be dragged to reach water. In the endeavor to get her off we sank in the soft, black mud nearly up to our knees, and found all our efforts vain. Coming out of the mud at last, in despair, with our trousers rolled up to our knees, we presented the appearance of a party of black legs.

"When will the tide rise again?" asked Jim Norton.

" Not till morning, I s'pose," replied Ben.

"Then we must stay here all night!"

This was a startling announcement.

"Why," said Ned Thompson, "to-morrow's Sunday!"

What would our parents say to our prolonged absence and our return on the Sabbath day? The thought gave us renewed energy, and we took another tug at the boat. She obstinately refused to move.

"Well," said Ben, "we can sleep in the barn."

This was a happy thought. It quite reconciled some of us to the prospect of remaining all night on the island. Sleeping in a barn was the very essence of romance and adventure. Had it not always been our ambition to do so on the night before the Fourth of July, and had not our request always been ruthlessly denied? Here was the chance thrust upon us. Were we to be blamed because the tide went out and left us?

Away we hurried to the barn and immediately

began heaping up the hay on the floor to make a bed. This done to our satisfaction, we sat down in the wide doorway and gazed upon the scene before us. The waters of the cove were as smooth as a mirror, reflecting in their depths its precipitous cliffs and the trees on their summits. The shades of evening, seeming to drop down from the tree-tops, began slowly to enclose the quiet scene. There was not a ripple on the water, not a sound in the air, no living thing stirring.

"How lonesome it is!" said Ned Thompson.

A homesick feeling was beginning to take possession of us, when we were startled by the sound of voices, and presently a boat rounded the northeastern end of Hog Island and entered the passage between Cow Island and Diamond Cove. There were two young men in it, and landing in the cove, they proceeded to take various articles from the boat. Then, while one built a fire on the rocks, the other busied himself in suspending two hammocks between trees.

"They are going to camp out," said Ben.

"Then we sha'n't be all alone here," remarked Ned Thompson, in a tone of relief.

We watched the dusky forms of the men as they moved about in front of their cheerful fire, busily engaged in preparing their evening meal. Presently they sat down to it, and as we saw them drinking their coffee and eating the food they had cooked, we began to have a hollow realization that our supper had been but a slight and unsatisfactory repast.

"I 'm awful hungry," said Si Sumner.

"Is n't there some of those biscuits left ?" inquired Joe.

"Not a crumb, But what 's become of that cake you were going to bring, Ned ?"

"Why," said Ned, with a sudden start of recollec-tion, " I forgot all about it.   I left it in the boat."

It was soon produced and scrupulously divided among us, but Si had taken but a mouthful when he said, with a dubious air, —

"Seems to me it tastes kind o' fishy.   Where did you find it, Tim ?"

"In the frying-pan in which we cooked the mack-erel."

"Pah !" said Ned, in a tone of disgust, " I can't eat it."

"Why," replied Tim, as he stowed away a huge slice of it, " it 's a good deal better than 'old horse,' such as Bill Truman had to eat."

"Well," said Ben, "plum-cake flavored with mack-erel is not to my taste."

However, most of us managed to dispose of our share of the cake, and felt all the better for it.

The moon had now risen, silvering the calm surface of the cove, and lighting up the leafy avenues at its head. We sat long contemplating the beauty of the scene, and conversing in low tones, as if we feared to disturb the repose of nature. It was a novel and awe-inspiring sensation to be alone on this uninhabited island in the silent watches of the night.

Presently we saw the two men on the opposite island rise from before their smouldering fire and betake themselves to their hammocks.

"Tell you what, boys," said Ben, "we'll come down here and camp out in vacation."

"Agreed!" cried we all.

"We can hire a sail-boat of -Johnny Leatherbee, and perhaps Bill Truman will come and manage it for us."

This was a happy thought, and under its inspiring influence we betook ourselves to our couch of hay on the barn floor. The hay was not abundant, and somehow the floor beneath it made its presence felt.

"I wish I had a pillow," said Ned Thompson.

"Put your arm under your head," said Joe, "and sleep on it. For my part I want a coverlid."

"Then," replied Ben, "you must pull down the roof of the barn."

That was indeed all between us and the sky, but fortunately the night was warm. Tired with the day's exertions, we soon fell asleep. Some time in the night I was awakened by Ned Thompson, who whispered, —

"Harry, there's somebody in the barn."

"I guess not," said I, but half awake, and scarcely conscious of my whereabouts.

"I heard them," replied Ned.

We lay still and listened. Presently I heard a rustling sound. Joe had evidently heard it, too, for he sat up and stared around. Soon the noise was repeated, and somehow I felt a strange sort of sinking in the region of my heart.

"Who's there?" asked Joe.

"Tu-whit, tu-whoo," was the reply, as a dark object flitted out of the door into the night.

"It's an owl," said Joe, as he lay down again.

Next morning we found our boat afloat, and made hasty preparations for departure, as we very much felt the need of getting a breakfast somewhere.

"We can row over to Mackey's Island, and get some bread and milk at the farm-house," said Joe.

This was agreed upon, and we were soon pulling across to Mackey's Island, which lay some distance inside of Hog Island. It was a dull, misty morning, and as we rowed away from Hog Island a fog bank came rolling in from the sea. The fog seemed to catch on the tree-tops and roll down from them in heavy masses, spreading itself over the surface of the water. Presently we were enveloped in it.

"Keep a good lookout for'ard," said Ben, who was rowing, "or else we'll miss the island."

After pulling a long time we held up and peered about us. Mackey's Island had disappeared in the fog. We listened, but heard no sound. After rowing on again for some time, with no signs of land, we again paused and listened.

"What was that?" said Ben. We had heard nothing, but presently a low, hollow sound struck upon our ears.

"It's a cow bellowing," said Ben; "row for it."

Guided by the lowing of the cow, which in our case supplied the place of the modern fog-horn, we soon struck the shore and found our way to the farm-house. A jolly-looking old man, half farmer, half fisherman, met us at the door.

"Good mornin', boys," said he, "ye're out airly."

"We would like to get some bread and milk," said Ben.

"Wall, walk right in. My daughter'll tend ter ye."

Bowls of milk with plenty of brown bread were soon supplied, and we fell to with ravenous appetites.

"Kinder got lost in the fog, did n't ye?" remarked the old man.

Ben replied that we had some difficulty in finding the island.

"Wall," continued our host, "fog is the beater-most thing. Ye never can find yer bearings in it. Did ye ever hear tell how old Sim Hooker, that lived on Peaks' Island, got lost in it? No? Wall, I'll tell ye how 't was. It was the curiousest thing ye ever heard on. Sim was n't over and above bright, and his ol' woman wus allus a jawing on him. Says she, 'Sim,' says she, 'you'll never set the river afire.' 'Lor-a-massy,' says Sim, 'I don't wanter; what ud become of us if all the water was burned up?' 'No danger on 't, no danger on 't,' says his wife.

"Wall, one day Sim wanted to go over to Bangs's Island to see ol' man Skillings about some lobster-pots he'd agreed to make for him. So he told the boys they might row him over and come back arter him in the arternoon. It was kinder foggy when they started, and putty soon the fog rolled in so thick over White Head ye might 'a' cut it with a knife. But the boys they knowed the bearings well enough, and arter rowing awhile they struck the island and landed the ol' man. He started for Skillings's house, but putty soon found hisself in a swamp that he never knowed was there afore. He thought it was kinder cur'us, but kep' flounderin' along till he got a'most up to his knees in mud and water.

"He could n't hardly see his hand afore his face, but he knowed Skillings's house could n't be fur off.

Bimeby he see a house looming up afore him, and he opened the door and went in. Arter he shut the door he thought things looked kinder nat'ral, and the fust thing he knowed there stood his ol' woman right afore him."

"'How 'd ye git here?' says he.

"'That's a putty question to ask,' says she. 'Have you lost your senses?'

"'Where on airth be I?' says he.

"'Why, ye ol' fool,' says she, 'ye 're in your own house, to be sure!'

"'How 'd I git here?' says Sim, kinder dazed like.

"'The Lord only knows, an' he won't tell,' says the ol' woman, 'but as fur as I can see ye got here on your own legs.'

"'But the boys jest landed me on Bangs's Island.'

"'Then ye must 'a' waded across White Head passige, an' I should think ye did by the looks o' your trousers!'

"Sim sat down by the fire, and tried to get the thing through his hair. At last he says, says he, —

"'Sally, them boys must 'a' landed me on the back side o' the island stid of on Bangs's Island.

"'Course they did,' says she, 'any fool might 'a' knowed that. But where on airth 's them boys?'

"'Sure enough!' says Sim, kinder starting up.

"'Who knows but they are rowing straight out to sea, an' you a setting here, bothering about how you got home. Go 'long down to the landin', do, says she, 'and git Jim Jackson to fire his gun, so 't them boys 'll know where they be.'

"So Sim he went down to the landin', and Jim got out his gun and was jest a going ter fire it off, when they heard the sound o' oars, and putty soon the boys rowed up to the wharf.

"'Where ye ben?' says Sim.

"'Over to Bangs's Island,' says they. It 'peared that arter they landed the ol' man they rowed away for home, as they thought, and putty soon they struck the shore, but could n't tell jest where they'd hit it. They see a man on shore, and they says to him, 'Where be we?' 'Ye're at Bangs's Island,' says he. And sure enough it was ol' man Skillings hisself. 'Where 's father?' says they. 'I hain't seed nothin' on him,' says Skillings. By that the boys was scart, and they pulled away for home for dear life.

"Ol' Sim he never could quite understand how 't was that when he started for Bangs's Island he got back to Peaks' without knowin' it, nor how 't was the boys who started for home arter they left him found theirselves at Bangs's Island afore they knowed it, but ye see it was all owing to the fog. It's the beatermost thing in all nater."

By noon the fog had cleared away and a strong breeze was kicking up a lively sea in the bay. We thought it time to start for home, but found it hard pulling against the tide and a heavy sea. Once or twice the waves dashed into the boat and gave us a drenching. Still we tugged at the oars by turns, but made little headway. Some of us began to grow a little disheartened. Presently a wave larger than common poured a flood of water into the boat, and we were obliged to set Tim and Ned at baling. Matters began to look a little serious with us.

"Boys," said Ben, "we'll never get round Fish Point. We'd better land back o' the Neck, and anchor the boat there until to-morrow morning."

This was agreed upon, and by keeping under the lee of the hill we were enabled to make better progress, and soon struck shoal water. The difficulty now was to secure the boat so that she would not go adrift during the night. The kellick was thrown out and loaded with stones, and everything on board made as snug as possible. Then we tucked up our trousers and waded ashore, Tim carrying his frying-pan for fear it would be stolen if left on board.

"Are you going to carry that through the streets on a Sunday?" asked Ned Thompson.

This was a reminder of the day that struck us all rather unpleasantly. We had landed at the extreme end of the town, and most of us must pass through more than half its length to reach our homes. However, by taking the back streets we got home without any unpleasant observations being made upon us. Next morning Ben Hunter and Jim Norton found the boat all right, and took her around to the brig in the harbor.

CHAPTER XIIL

IN CAMP.

IN July we had two weeks vacation. We did not forget our determination to spend it in camp at Diamond Cove. In fact, some of us had been preparing for it ever since our trip down the bay. Joe Jameson, whose uncle was in the Blues, had procured for us the loan of a tent. We had saved up our pocket-money to purchase stores.

"We must have plenty of biscuit," said Ben.

"And some pork," added Tim, remembering his experience in frying mackerel.

"And don't forget potatoes; they are jolly good roasted in the ashes," said Si Sumner.

Supplies laid in, the next thing was to hire a sail-boat. Bill Truman had promised to go along and manage it for us, although by this time Ben Hunter considered himself competent to take the helm.

"Give me your names, boys," said Johnny Leatherbee, when we appeared before him to engage the boat. "If you are all drowned I shall have to report ye."

This was a damper on our high spirits. We had n't thought of drowning. But then we remembered that boats had been capsized by sudden squalls in Diamond Cove, and that a number of lives had been lost in that way.

"Don't you worry about our drowning, Johnny," said Bill Truman. "I 'm going skipper of this craft."

"Well," replied Johnny, "I s'pose them that 's born to be hanged will never be drowned. You 're safe enough."

With this comforting assurance we proceeded down the wharf, each one carrying his share of the stores. On the way we met several officers from the fort, in full uniform. They were fine, stately looking men, and walking very sedately with them was the young soldier boy who had been our guide at the fort. Several of us made signs of recognition, but he gave us a look which plainly indicated that he could not acknowledge our acquaintance in such a presence. I never met him again, but I have sometimes thought of him as in high command in the army. He evidently had the making of a soldier in him.

Before a stiff breeze our boat was soon dancing over the waves, and the spirit of adventure took full possession of us. Ben proposed that we should penetrate the unknown region of the lower bay, even as

far as Harpswell, but Bill Truman said we should
have to beat back and might not get to the cove
until late in the day. We therefore contented ourselves with making a stop at Peaks' Island and calling on Mrs. Stirling. The old lady stood in the
doorway shading her eyes with her hand.

"Sakes alive, boys, is 't you?" said she. "How
you hev growed. I should n't 'a' knowed ye. Come
right in, all on ye, and take some cheers."

Jim Norton introduced our companions, and men-
tioned our purpose of camping at Diamond Cove.

"So ye 're going to camp out, be ye? Wall, ye 'll
find it rough living, but I s'pose ye 'll like it for a
spell, if ye can git enough to eat," she added dubiously. "But if ye get short o' vittles come right
over here an' I 'll supply ye."

At this moment Susie entered, looking fresh and
rosy. She said she thought it would be fun camping
out in the cove, and when I politely invited her to
visit us she promised to do so.

On arriving in the cove we found no one there,
and rejoiced in having it all to ourselves. With much
bustle and excitement we landed our stores and proceeded to pitch the tent on a dry knoll, taking care
to fasten the stays strongly to pegs driven firmly into
the ground.

"We must dig a channel around the tent," said

Joe Jameson, who had camped out with his uncle on one occasion, "to carry off the water when it rains."

"And we must make a bed of fir boughs," said B ·

We set about gathering the boughs, and Jim Norton undertook to spread them on the ground inside the tent.

"That won't do," said Joe, critically examining his work, "you must use only the small twigs, and lay the stems all one way, or else you'll feel as if you were lying on a gridiron."

The boughs were rearranged smoothly, and with the old coverlid Tim Bunce had brought along, they made a very comfortable bed

Meanwhile Bill Truman was busy anchoring the boat off in the cove, coming ashore in the small row-boat we had brought in tow.

"Now, boys," said Ben Hunter, "we must divide the work, and there must be no shirks here. Harry, you must be tent-keeper, and see that everything is kept snug inside; Jim, you must be water-carrier; Si, you must be fireman; Joe, you must be potato-slicer and dish-washer; Tim and I will be cooks, and Bill will look after the boat and go a fishing."

There was some grumbling at this autocratic distribution of the work. Joe declared he wouldn't be dish-washer, and Jim grumbled at having to lug water from the spring. Si said he was a dabster at washing dishes, and offered to swap places with Joe, which arrangement was satisfactorily made.

Everything being set in order, we took a stroll in the leafy alleys behind our tent. The wood here was a thick growth, tangled with underbrush and fallen tree-trunks, but the paths running through them were delightfully embowered and bordered with ferns and running vines. There was a mixed growth of evergreen and deciduous trees, and among the latter were numerous sturdy, wide-spreading beeches. The smooth trunks of these were cut deep with the initials of former visitors, some of them bearing date of many years previous. In these cases the letters were spread wide with the growth of the bark, and in a few instances were almost obliterated.

These beeches were large in circumference, the gnarled and twisted branches growing low and spreading out almost at right angles with the stem. They made leafy coverts, under which we lingered long, reading the names cut on their stems, sometimes spelled out at length, sometimes merely initials, and occasionally those of youth and maiden, lovingly coupled with a brace.

"Do you s'pose these people are all dead?" asked Ned, to whom the inscriptions seemed to have a sort of graveyard aspect.

"I know one of 'em is n't," replied Ben, "but he 's gone to the East Indies, and he 's never coming back. He came down here the day before he sailed, and cut his name there," pointing to some deeply cut letters on the tree under which he stood. "He said he wanted to leave his name somewhere in his native city, and he had rather leave it here, where he had enjoyed so many good times picnicking and camping out." We looked with much interest at the letters, "J. S., 1830."

Returning to camp, we set about preparing our evening meal. Jim trudged off to the spring for water; Joe had providentally brought an armful of dry sticks from the woods, and soon had a cheerful blaze in the stone fireplace. Ben placed a pot of coffee on the fire, while Si put some potatoes to roast beneath it, and Tim got out the biscuit and butter.

What a jolly feast· it was when all was ready. Do you recall the ·time, O widely scattered Landsport boys ! when you sat around the fire on the grassy bank of Diamond or Pleasant Cove, and ate your chowder or fried fish, and have you ever, in all your wanderings, tasted food so delicious, or with so keen an appetite ?

We sat long about the smudge made to drive off the mosquitoes, discussing plans for the coming days. We were to go out fishing, perhaps take a cruise down the bay, go berrying on the island, and dig clams on the bar connecting Great Hog with Little Hog Island.

Si Sumner had made a separate couch for himself in a corner of the tent. The night was warm, and on retiring early, Si thought it would be a good thing to entirely disrobe himself. Presently he leaped from his couch with loud exclamations of impatience and distress.

"What's the matter?" we all exclaimed.

"The mosquitoes are devouring me."

"Put on your shirt," said Ben.

This was a happy thought, immediately acted upon by Si, but the mosquitoes were not to be so easily baffled. Those of Diamond Cove were a famous race. They were large, ferocious, and their name was legion. They had put to flight more than one party of campers. We soon heard Si thrashing his arms about his head, where the enemy were loudly buzzing.

"Pull up your coverlid," said Joe, sitting comfortably in the smoke of the smudge.

"It's too short. When I pull it up, my feet stick out, and then they go for them."

"Put on your boots," suggested Bill.

"So I will," said Si; "I never thought of that."

Defeated at one extremity, the mosquitoes renewed the attack at the other, and made an onslaught about his head. Si was now forced to put on his cap, and was finally compelled to protect his body by donning his overcoat. Thus defended, he lay down to his repose, and after that night never retired without first putting on his overcoat and pulling it well up in the neck.

At last we all stretched ourselves on the boughs in the tent and pulled the coverlid over us. We were tired and soon fell asleep. Some time in the night I was awakened by a strange noise that sounded like a screech close at my ear. I listened, and presently the sound was repeated. This time it seemed like the scream of a wild animal.

"What's that?" whispered Si Sumner, who lay next me.

"I don't know," said I, "perhaps it's the wind." It had risen in the night.

By this time the whole tent was awake, and all were listening for the strange noise, which came again, a most uncanny screech.

"It's something right back of the tent," said Joe.

"I'll soon see what it is," said Tim, who was not easily frightened. He crawled out of the tent, and, as he did so, the strange, unearthly sound came again, making all our hearts quake. Nothing daunted, Tim went back of the tent, and soon returned laughing.

"I 've found the ghost," said he, "it 's nothing but the branch of a bush that the wind scrapes against the tent. I broke it off, and the ghost is laid."

When we awoke next morning the sun was high in the heavens. How delicious was the morning air as we emerged from the tent and performed our ablutions at the spring!

It was decided to have a chowder for dinner that day, and Bill Truman and Tim Bunce went out to catch the fish, while those who remained engaged in a game of quoits. When the fishermen returned with a fine cod and a few mackerel, Ben Hunter, who prided himself on his knowledge of cookery, set about preparing the chowder.

When dinner was announced each one appeared with his bowl and improvised spoon, made of a clamshell with a split stick for a handle. The chowder did n't taste like that Mrs. Stirling set before Jim and me the morning after we came off the ice. After swallowing a spoonful Tim Bunce remarked, —

"This is an awful flat chowder."

"I 've found a scrap of pork in mine," said Ned Thompson, who hated pork.

"Did you put the pork scraps in the chowder?" asked Tim.

"To be sure I did," replied Ben. "What else should I do with them ?"

" And what did you do with the pork fat ? "

" Threw it away, of course."

" That 's the kind of a cook you are," replied Tim, in great disgust. " Don't you know you ought to have thrown the scraps away and put the fat into the chowder ? That 's what makes it rich and good."

A hot dispute ensued between Ben and Tim, while the rest of us gave our attention to the chowder, which was made palatable by hunger. Camping out had given us all a ravenous appetite. The remainder of the chowder was set aside for breakfast. When we attacked it next morning it was of the consistency of hasty pudding. Ben had been stirring it over the fire with a stick, and as the pot had stood over night under a pine-tree, the spills that had fallen into it had been well mixed in.

" It looks like mortar," said Ned, in a tone of disgust, refusing to eat it.

It was unanimously voted that the chowder was not a success, though Ben still contended that he was right about the pork.

Some time after breakfast a boat was seen approaching the cove. Mr. Stirling was rowing, while Miss Susie sat in the stern.

" Hurry, boys," said I, "and clean up the camp. Visitors are coming."

Jim Norton especially bestirred himself to put

everything in order, and took care to be at the shore to assist Susie in landing.

"Boys," said Mr. Stirling, "I've brought ye some fish. I thought p'r'aps ye'd like to make a chowder."

Tim Bunce made one of his sly grimaces, which set us all laughing.

"We have tried to make a chowder," said Joe, "but did not succeed very well."

"I don't s'pose ye did," replied the old man. "Boys ginerally don't know much about cooking. But here's Susie, she'll make a chowder for ye fit for the king."

Susie laughed heartily when told about Ben's throwing away the pork fat, and Ned comparing the chowder to mortar. She expressed her willingness to instruct us in the art of chowder-making, and we all set about assisting her with a will.

Under her directions water was put to boil in a tin dipper over a side fire. Then some slices of pork were put into the frying-pan, Susie telling us to be careful that they were not burned, as that would give the chowder a dark color and disagreeable flavor.

Si, as potato-slicer, was set at peeling and slicing the potatoes and onions. From among the fish he had brought Mr. Stirling selected a fine, fresh haddock, remarking that its flesh was firmer than that of the cod, and that it made a better chowder. It must not be sliced, Susie added, but cut into large pieces.

When all was ready, the hot pork fat was poured into the kettle first of all, care being taken, this time, not to put in the scraps, much to the content-ment of Tim and the chagrin of Ben. Then a layer of sliced potatoes was put in and on this a layer of sliced onions, with hard bread crumbled in, and the whole seasoned with pepper and salt. Next a por-tion of the fish was added and on this other layers of potatoes and onions with more pepper and salt. Then more fish, taking care that it was not broken up. Next the boiling water was poured in, and the whole set to boil until the potatoes were done, Susie testing them with a fork.

Meantime a can of milk, which Mr. Stirling had providently provided, had been set on the fire and its contents were now poured into the kettle. Last of all, a piece of butter was added, and the chowder was done. It was a delicious dish, and Susie was given a unanimous vote of thanks for her instruction in the preparation of it.

As we sat around the cloth spread upon the ground, which served as a table, Ben asked Mr. Stirling how far it was to Jewell's Island, as we had some intention of visiting it.

"It's on'y about six miles from here," replied the old man, "but, boys, don't ye be too ventersome. Thet's partly what I kim over for, to warn ye. I've never felt skeersly right about boys camping out here alone sense them three boys was lost, nigh on ten years ago."

"Tell us about it," said Ben, while the rest of us drew near to listen.

"Wall, ye see, it was a terrible onlucky thing. My ol' woman never could git over it. Says she to me, on'y yisterday, says she, 'Do go over an'. tell them boys not to go cruising down the bay.' A.' thet's partly why I kim over. Ye see three likely boys kim down here one summer and was camping out, jest as you be now. They used ter come over to the house arter milk and things, an' my wife she took quite a shine to 'em.

"Well, they used to go cruising round in their boat, an' I never thought no harm on 't, though I might 'a' knowed they could n't manage the boat in a stiff breeze. One day I was out fishing, an' I see towards night it was a comin' in thick, so I pulled up kellick and stood away fer home. Afore long it begun to rain and blow, an' kim on pretty rough. By the time I got into Hussey's Sound it was as dark and dirty as ever I see it. Jest then I see a boat driving past; and somebody aboard sung out something, but the wind was a screeching so I could n't hear what he said, and in a half a minute the boat was out ev sight. I hed es much es I would do to tend to my own boat, and did n't think no more of it, 'specially as I thought the boat belonged to some of the Long-Islanders, who was making for home, es I was.

"Wall, two days afterwards a man kim to my house an' asked if I 'd seen anything o' them boys that had been camping out in the cove. He said they did n't come home at the time sot, an' he 'd been over to the cove, and found their camp de-sarted. 'What day was it they was comin' home?' says I. 'Day before yisterday,' says he. Then it come over me like a shot it was them boys that drove by me in the storm. I could n't say a word at fust, but tol' the man — he was the father of one of 'em — that I guessed he would find 'em on Long Island. I kinder hoped they 'd landed there. But nothing more was ever heard of 'em, an' I s'pose I was the last one that seed 'em alive. So now, boys, I warn ye to be keerful. Don't ye go cruising about, 'specially if it looks like thick weather coming on "

We thanked the old man for his kindly caution, and promised to profit by it.

"For all that," said Ben, after he and Susie had departed, "I guess we can venture down to Jewell's Island, if we take a fair day for it."

That night, as we lay asleep in the tent, we were awakened by a heavy clap of thunder. Presently the rain poured down in torrents, and flash after flash of vivid lightning revealed the whole cove, as if by a magical illumination. As I lay in the tent I could look out of the narrow opening in the flap and see the inside of the barn on Cow Island lighted up for a moment, and then hidden again in impenetrable darkness. Fortunately, our tent shed the water well, only a thin mist penetrating it, and the channel we had dug around it carried off the torrent that fell from it.

"Harry," said Si to me, in a whisper, "where's that flask of powder Ben brought down? If the lightning should strike the tent it might blow us all up."

"Here it is," said I; whereupon Si seized it and threw it as far out of the tent as he could.

The shower soon passed over, and next morning Ben was making great inquiry for his powder-flask. He had brought down a gun with the avowed purpose of supplying the camp with game, but as yet had shot nothing except an owl, which Tim said would make a dish equal to Ben's chowder. The flask was found, but though Ben diligently tramped through the woods, gun in hand, he made no contribution to our larder.

In fact, our supplies began to fail, and famine
stared us in the face. The hardships of camp life
began to bring out traits of character not before suspected. Jim proved to be lazy, and neglected to
keep the camp supplied with water; Joe shirked his
duty as fireman, and Si grumbled at having to wash
dishes in cold water. Somehow he could n't get the
grease off. Ben and Tim proved the truth of the
old proverb that " Too many cooks spoil the broth,"
since they were continually quarrelling about the
proper way of cooking our food, and between them
spoiled everthing they undertook. . Bill proved to
be a good provider in the way of catching fish, and
but for him we might have starved. Ned was homesick. As the shades of evening drew on, and we
sat at the tent door in the solitary cove, he would
say, "To-morrow morning, boys, I 'm going home."
With the morning sun, and the arrival of picnicking
parties, his courage revived, and he would postpone
his departure until the next day. As for myself, I
found it more agreeable to row about the cove in the
small boat than to keep the camp in order.

One day, when our supplies had run very low, and
it had become a serious question whether we should
be able to provide anything for dinner, I saw a boy
approaching the camp through one of the shady
paths leading to the other end of the island, where

there was a farm-house. He had come to say that his father desired our help in getting in his hay, as he feared a shower was approaching. The farmer had probably a suspicion that food was not very abundant with us, as he offered as a consideration to give us a good dinner at the farm-house.

"Good for you," said Tim Bunce, in answer to the proposition. "I'm the boy for getting in hay."

We all eagerly accepted the offer in anticipation of food and fun, and hurried away through the woods to the hay-field, a mile distant. There was much fun in raking the hay and treading it in the hay-rack, and when the last load drove into the barn, just as the rain began to fall, we were all ready for dinner.

It was a hearty meal that the farmer's wife set before us, and we did it full justice. Corned beef and cabbage and Indian pudding had become luxuries, and it was a novelty to be sitting at a table and eating from clean dishes. The farmer's wife hospitably urged us to partake of everything on the table.

"Now take right hold, boys, and help yourselves," said she. "I know this camping out makes boys hungry."

We had found that out long before, and were not slow in accepting her invitation, Tim declaring in an aside that he was going to eat enough to last a week.

14

It continued to rain through the afternoon, and at night we found it necessary to close the tent and make everything snug. About the witching hour of midnight some of us were awakened by a heavy tramping, and presently some object was hurled against the tent with such vigorous and repeated blows as to break its fastenings and throw it down upon us. We were all buried beneath it, and some of us who were scarcely awake had difficulty in disentangling ourselves. Joe backed out heels foremost, as we all shouted, —

"Who did it?"

Nobody knew, but Bill said that when he emerged from the tent he saw a white object dashing away through the woods.

"Do you s'pose it was a ghost?" whispered Ned.

"Nonsense," replied Ben,. "I'll tell you what it was, — the farmer's old white horse."

And so it proved to be. The horse had been turned loose, and wandering through the woods had caught sight of our tent. So strange an object had excited his fears or animosity, and turning tail he had given it a succession of vigorous kicks, with the result above described.

It was still raining and it was very dark. We could not see to replace the tent and must seek other shelter. There was nothing for it but a long tramp through the woods and fields to the farm-house. On the way Si and Ned wandered out of the path and fell into the swamp. Their cries drew us all back, but in the darkness we wandered in different directions and only by much shouting were enabled to come together again.

Having fished poor Ned out of the swamp, we set out again, but soon found ourselves on the shore, and it was only after much wandering about that we at last reached the farm-house. Here it required much thumping and shouting to awaken the family. When at last admitted, thoroughly drenched, we gave a doleful account of our disaster.

" Ye must put up the bars, boys," said the farmer· "Old Whitey never see a tent before and he was bound to know what was in it."

" He'll find out if he comes prowling about again," said Tim.

The farmer's wife stowed us away in spare beds and improvised couches on the floor, where we slept soundly until morning.

Some days after our midnight adventure, our supply of biscuit having been exhausted, it became necessary to send up to town for more. All were eager to go, and it was at last determined that only the camp-keeper should remain. As I held that responsible office I was left alone in the cove.

It was understood that the supply party would remain in town over night. I therefore prepared for a lonely vigil and made all snug about the camp. Feeling rather lonesome as the afternoon wore away, I thought to amuse myself by rowing off to Crow Island in the small boat. Crow Island was a little nubble rising high out of the water not far from the entrance to the cove.

After rambling over it for some time I went down on to a bit of sandy beach in a little cove and observed near low-water mark a number of small objects thrust up out of the sand. These were razor shells, long, narrow shell-fish, which sink vertically into the sand, foot downward. As I approached them the vibration of the sand under my feet gave them the alarm and they sank out of sight in the twinkling of an eye. Retreating to the shore, I was amused to observe them, after a short time, slowly obtruding themselves again, as if cautiously looking around for the enemy. Advancing softly this time, I was enabled to seize two of them and pull them out of the sand. With a bit of board found on the beach I dug up a number of them. They were about six inches long, but some of their burrows were two feet deep.

After amusing myself some time in this way, and the shades of evening beginning to fall, I bethought me of returning to the cove. Passing over the nubble to the point where I had left the boat, I was startled to find no boat there. I had passed the painter around a bowlder on the shore, and the movement of the boat in rising and falling with the waves had worked it loose. Looking over the water, I saw the boat dancing away towards Cow Island. As it rose and fell it seemed to be nodding me good-by.

Here was a situation! It was bad enough to be left alone in the camp, but to spend the night without shelter on Cow Island was more than I had bargained for. Various expedients suggested themselves to me, but none were practicable. It was too far for me to swim ; there was nothing on the island of which to construct a raft, and no sail was in sight to come to my rescue. There was nothing to be done but to prepare for a night in the open air.

On the summit of the nubble there was a little grassy hollow. In this I placed some sea-weed which had been thrown up on the beach and dried in the sun, and thus made a sort of nest in which I hoped to shelter myself.

This done, I felt the need of something to eat. I had brought no luncheon with me, but had a few matches in my pocket. With these I kindled a fire of driftwood, and when it had burned down I placed the razor-shells on the hot stones. I had never eaten these shell-fish, but had heard of others doing so.

The shells gaped open under the influence of the heat, and when I thought they were done to a turn I attempted to swallow one. It was a feat not easily accomplished with only the aid of my fingers in tearing it from the shell, but it went down at last, and proved not altogether unpalatable. I ate several of them, and then bethought me of the mussels on the shore, a quantity of which I gathered and served in the same way.

By this time the starlit evening was far advanced. I sought my nest, but found it did not invite to slumber. I lay long awake, gazing into the starry heavens, and listening to the *lap, lap* of the waves on the shore. The night was calm and the sea was smooth. No sail was in sight, yet I fancied boats were approaching. I seemed to hear the oars in the rowlocks, and the low voices of men conversing. Then I started up and listened, but all was still. I tried to compose myself to sleep again, but the night air coming in from the sea was chilly, and my slumber was broken and disturbed by troublous dreams.

I got up and walked about for a time in the endeavor to keep warm; then lay down again and dozed. Presently I became aware of some presence about me. It seemed to be approaching, and in a moment more it pounced down upon me, like some great bird of prey about to bear me away. When I was fully awakened and recovered from my fright I became aware that it was one of the sheep pastured on the island, which in wandering about had stumbled over me. .

I lay down again, and when I awoke the day was breaking. I wandered down by the shore and built a fire, and waited long for my companions. Sail after sail appeared in sight, went past, and left me disappointed. I was hungry and angry. They had promised to return early in the morning. Why did they not come?

Late in the forenoon I at last saw them in the distance. I knew it was them because Tim Bunce's red head shone out resplendant in the bow. I saw them enter the cove. Then a revulsion of feeling came over me. I was in no hurry to quit my solitary isle. I would punish them for lingering on their return. They should look in vain for me. I enjoyed seeing them land, hurry up to the tent, look around, and call for "Harry." No Harry appeared. At length they seemed to be alarmed. Several went into the woods to look for me, while others skirted the shore. They ran to and fro and called aloud. At last one of them spied the small boat drifting away from Cow Island, where it had gone ashore in the night. Now they thought I must be drowned, and there were loud shouts of alarm and great haste in embarking in pursuit of the drifting boat. Then I stood up and shouted, and there was great wonder at my sudden appearance on the solitary nubble.

When we all sat around the bountiful breakfast provided by Tim, there was great inquiry concerning my adventure and much laughter at my fright by the sheep.

"Did you think it was a bear?" asked Ned.

"Why did n't you kill the sheep, and have roast mutton for breakfast?" inquired Ben.

"Any way, we know where we can get some fresh meat now, when we want it," remarked Si.

"There is n't one of you that has pluck enough to kill a sheep," said Bill.

"We'll appoint you butcher, you are so brave," retorted Si.

"No need of a butcher, boys, with all this grub on hand," remarked Ben. "See, Harry, what your grandmother sent you down."

There were a roasted chicken and great stores of bread, cake, and oranges. We feasted royally that day.

That afternoon it was proposed to go over to Cow Island, where there was a cleared field, and play a game of ball. We were to go over in the small row-boat, and Joe suggested that if we all stood up the boat would take us all at one trip. Being tent-keeper, and having to make things snug before leaving, I was the last to enter the boat. As I did so I saw that the pressure of so many feet in the small boat had started the bottom and the water was pouring in. I immediately sprang ashore, exclaiming, —

"Look out, boys, she's going down."

The impetus given to the boat by my leap sent her off from the shore, and immediately she filled and sank, immersing her occupants up to their necks. There was a great scrambling on shore, the boys coming up dripping, and in great wrath and indignation at my having pushed off the boat. Tim proposed to flog me on the spot, but Ben shouted, —

"Now you hustle round and get some wood for a fire."

I accordingly made myself busy in gathering firewood, and soon had a lively blaze around which my companions stood and turned themselves about, like so many geese roasting before the fire. At short intervals the order was given for more firewood, in a tone that implied that the gathering of it was the least I could do to atone for giving them a ducking. As they dried off, however, their wrath evaporated with the water from their clothing, and when we had eaten our supper Tim was ready to treat the catastrophe as a good joke. Ben said they were all in a pretty pickle, whereupon Tim remarked, —

"Yes, and I never liked souse."

The next day proving fair, with a favorable breeze, it was resolved to put in execution our long-contemplated plan of a cruise to Jewell's Island. This was one of the outer islands of the bay, about which there were many tales told of treasures hidden there by the pirates in the times gone by. It was said that Capt. Kidd had secreted there a portion of the ill-gotten gains he scattered so far and wide about the world. Many had dug there for treasure, but though there were mysterious whisperings about what had been found, no one had positive knowledge of success in the search.

"Suppose we were lucky enough to find the treasure," said Si, "what would we do with it?"

"We'd build a ship and go cruising around the world," replied Jim, who had always a hankering for the sea.

"No," said Joe, "we'd set up a stage-coach line, and all turn drivers." Joe was much in his father's stable and had an ambition to handle the ribbons.

"I would travel in foreign lands," said Ben.

"And I," added Ned, "would build a big house and live at my ease."

"No doubt of that, lazy-bones," replied Ben.

We were now sailing past Hope Island, which presented a high green shore sloping up to a crown of dense woods. The islands thickened at the bottom of the bay like plums in the end of a pudding. Some were low and rocky, others rose like hills out of the sea. Eagle Island, in the mouth of Broad Sound, stood high and darkly wooded. Outside of Hope Island lay Crotch Island, and beyond that Jewell's.

We entered a deep cove made by a point of land running out from the shore. At the head of it, on a high, green bank, stood the one house on the island, long occupied by a retired sea-captain, who was always on hand to receive trespassers with a growl. No dogs could be allowed to land because of his sheep. No fires must be built on the island. But if you got on the right side of him he was not uncommunicative, and would relate the traditions of the island and the adventures of the money-diggers.

On this occasion he proved a good Samaritan to us. The wind had freshened and suddenly chopped around as we entered the cove. We dropped anchor, but it did not hold, and presently we found ourselves driving on to the rocky shore, where the boat would inevitably beat to pieces. We were in some alarm, when we saw the captain and his son putting off from the shore in a small boat. They came on board with a line, one end of which they made fast to a small schooner lying in the cove, and we were thus enabled to pull the boat into a place of safety.

Landing on the beach, we climbed the high bank, in the side of which we saw a deep hole.

"Is that where the treasure was found?" asked Ned, who was always the first to make inquiries.

"That's where they dug," replied the old captain, dryly.

"How do you s'pose the treasure came there?"

"I've hearn tell it was hid by pirates," was the non-committal reply.

We wandered to the outer end of the island, where, under the freshening gale, the sea was breaking high on the rocky shore. The ocean lay broad off, and the big waves came tumbling in and leaping into foam on the rocks. Venturing out too far, a larger wave than usual broke completely over Ben and Joe, and nearly swept them away.

We retreated in all haste, and as the gale was evidently increasing, we determined to remain on the island all night. The captain said gruffly that he guessed he could accommodate us. Any way, it wasn't safe for us boys to attempt to go up the bay in that boat.

At the supper table brown sugar was served, but the captain's wife said, —

"Perhaps the boys would like white sugar."

"What's good enough for me is good enough for them that eat at my table," growled the old sea-dog.

We all hastened to say that we didn't care for white sugar.

After supper, as we sat in the low-roofed room, while the wind rattled the loose windows, the captain became more genial and communicative. One of us remarking on the storm, he said, —

"This ain't nothing to what we get here sometimes. I remember when a fishing schooner went ashore, and three men were drowned. She put in here in the arternoon, and it was a threatening sky, and I told 'em bad weather was ahead, but they said they must be off and make for Monhegan. Afore they was under way snow began to fall and the wind freshened. I went to bed, but woke up from a bad dream. I'd seen the schooner heading on the rocks and heard the cries of the crew. I couldn't sleep, so I dressed myself and took my lantern, and went to the outer shore, where I'd seen the vessel in my dream.

"Sure enough, there she was. It was a thick night, but in a lull of the storm I could see the schooner swinging on the rocks, and could hear the shouts of the poor fellers aboard of her. But I couldn't do nothing. No boat could live in that sea. I watched till I see her go to pieces, and in the morning I found three dead bodies washed ashore, and I buried 'em on the p'int where the vessel struck."

We sat silent for a time after this sad tale, and listened to the wind still rattling the windows and howling around the corners of the house. Presently Ned said, —

"Do you believe the pirates ever landed here?"

"Likely's not, likely's not," was the reply. "I know there was pirates in them days, for I've had a tussle with 'em myself."

Thereupon the captain bared his breast, and showed us the scar of a wound which he said had been inflicted by the knife of a pirate in the days when he followed the sea. We looked upon him with a mingled feeling of awe and admiration after that.

"Did you ever find any of the treasure the pirates hid here?" asked Joe.

"Can't say I ever did," was the dry reply, "but I've seen them that said they did. There was a feller came down here that said he was guided by sperits, and he dug, and he dug, and one night, arter he'd spent all his money, he slipped away, and they do say he took with him a bushel and a half of old Spanish dollars. But I never see any of 'em. I allus let 'em dig, and never refused to sell 'em nothing that they wanted."

This was said with a grim smile that led me to conclude that the captain made more out of the diggers than they did out of the hidden treasure.

In the morning we were shown a square hole cut in the rock by drill and blast, the size of a chest, where the captain said he found pieces of iron which had lain, covered with rust, no one knew how many years.

After paying the captain for our lodging we took leave of him, and the gale having blown itself out in the night, we had a pleasant passage back to the cove.

Not intending to remain away over night, we had made everything snug and closed the tent, but left no one in charge. On landing I observed that the camp had a disordered look. Various articles that I had put snugly away were scattered about. Tim's frying-pan was hanging on the branch of a tree. The chowder-kettle was turned over the top of a stump. Another stump was dressed up in Bill's old red flannel shirt, the arms extended wide by two branches thrust through them, while on top of all was Ben's old cap. This scare-crow was labelled in a scrawling hand, —

" Camp-keeper, — on guard ! "

We all rushed to the tent. Ben was the first to enter, and taking a look around, came out again, shouting, —

" Thieves ! thieves ! "

An examination of the premises made it only too

evident that during our absence a gang of maraud‚
ers had made free with our possessions.   Various
articles were missing and everything was turned
topsy-turvy.

"The pirates have made a descent upon us while
we were visiting their old haunt," said I.

"And they've stolen my gun," said Ben.

"Lucky for us," replied Bill, who had no great
faith in Ben's marksmanship.

"I say, Harry, they made a capital likeness of
you," said Joe, pointing to the effigy of the "Camp-
keeper."

On the whole we rather enjoyed the adventure of
being robbed.   It strengthened our faith in the
pirates and their treasure.   But when Tim, who had
set about preparing dinner, cried out, —

"Where's the grub?" and it became evident after
long search that the thieves had cleared the camp of
everything eatable, the raid did not seem so amusing.
We began to pull very long faces.

"Haven't they left anything?" asked Jim.

"Not a blessed crumb!"

"There's nothing for it but to go clam-digging,"
said Bill.

"I won't dig clams," replied Ned.

"Well, I'm getting tired of it, anyway," said Si;
"let's go home."

If the truth were known, I suspect we were all glad of this suggestion, though few of us cared to be the first to make it. We had exhausted the pleasures of camping out for the time being, and were glad to return to the comforts of home.

By the time we were under sail the afternoon was far advanced, and a fog-bank had come rolling in from the sea. Bill was at the helm, and we trusted to his knowledge of the harbor. After beating about for a long time, the fog slightly lifted and we beheld a white tower rising on the rocky shore close at hand.

" Landsport Light!" cried Ben, "we 're going out to sea. Put her about!"

We were, indeed, just leaving the entrance of the harbor and launching out into the broad Atlantic. The discovery was timely, and Bill lost no time in putting about, and we beat slowly up the harbor, landing at Commercial Wharf as the Second Parish bell was ringing for 9 o'clock P. M.

CHAPTER XIV.

WE JOURNEY TO A FAR COUNTRY.

ONE bright morning in the summer succeeding that of our camping out at Diamond Cove, I met Jim Norton in front of the Elm Tavern. I had not seen him in a long time. In fact, we boys had seldom met of late. We had come to the parting of the ways. The Liberty Street Lancers were disbanded. Capt. Ben had removed from the town; Bill Truman had sailed on a long voyage; Tim Bunce had been put at the carpenter's trade; Joe Jameson had been sent to New Orleans to find there the pursuit of his life; Jim Norton lived at the lower end of the town and I met him but seldom.

On this fair summer morning we had both been attracted to the Elm Tavern to witness the departure of the stage-coaches. It was a bustling scene. The coaches running on the various lines, after picking up their passengers about town, came dashing up to the tavern to take those who were stopping there. At times there were half a dozen of them at the doors, each drawn by four horses. The loading of

the baggage, the seating of the passengers, the fare-
wells of friends, the cracking of whips, and the final
departure made a spectacle often witnessed by an
idle crowd.

Among these well-filled vehicles was John Smith's
White Mountain stage-coach.   It had an awning
spread over the top, under which were seats, and was
thus known as a "double-decker."   Gay parties leaving for the mountains climbed eagerly to these upper
seats.

With what joyousness they set off, merry shouts
and laughter floating back from them.   Did any one,
I wonder, ever take his seat in a railroad car, at the,
outset of a pleasure trip, with anything like the exhilaration of spirits he experienced on his first ride
on a stage-coach?   The pure, sweet, morning air,
the elevation of the seat, giving a commanding view
of the road and the country around ; the spirited action of the horses, the sense of motion, as if one
were flying through the air, — what has the rail to
compensate for the loss of these?

"Jim," said I, "would n't it be a jolly thing if *we*
could go to the White Mountains?"

"Perhaps we can go.   I 've just been thinking
how we might do it.   Vacation begins next week,
and my uncle is coming down from Norway with his
own team and is going to leave it here while he takes

a trip to Boston. He will have to board his horse at a livery stable, and I believe he will be glad, rather than be at that expense, to let the team to us for a small sum."

"Good!" said I, and we parted with the understanding that, if possible, this plan for an excursion should be carried out.

A few days later, Jim came to say that his uncle had arrived and had agreed to let us his team for a week for the sum of seven dollars. The next step was to provide for the other expenses of the journey.

"We can carry our own grub," said Jim.

"Yes, and we can stop at some roadside spring and eat it under the shade of the trees," replied I, charmed with the romantic aspect of the trip. "And the first night we can stop at my aunt's house in Bankville."

This town was not on the direct route to the mountains, but could be reached in a day's drive, with but a slight divergence.

On the appointed morning we set out in high spirits. Our way lay through the country towns, where the farmers were busy in the fields, and the air was filled with the fragrance of new-mown hay. At noon we stopped beside a bubbling spring, under a wide-spreading maple, and ate our dinner with great relish.

Late in the afternoon we drove into the little village of Bankville.   There were a tavern and several shops on the main street.   In front of these were a number of loiterers, who stared at us curiously as we passed.   They appeared to be a jolly if not a tipsy crowd.   Two men, one wearing a cobbler's apron, and the other having the appearance of a blacksmith, were engaged in a hot dispute in front of one of the shops.   On the roof of the shop, which sloped down towards the rear, a young fellow was clambering, unseen by them, with a bucket of water in his hand.   Creeping slyly to the front, he emptied the water upon the heads of the tipsy disputants, and then slid rapidly from the roof in the rear.   The sudden douche cooled the ardor of the wranglers, but set them to swearing, while a loud laugh went up from the idlers around.

The next object that attracted our attention, as we drove on, was a crockery crate, near one of the shop doors, under which lay a youth in a drunken stupor, while a placard on the crate indicated that he was on exhibition, — "price ten cents a peep."

Bankville was evidently a hilarious town.   My aunt resided in a large white house at the farther end of the village.   We met with a hearty welcome, and my cousin, a boy of about my own age, gave us a graphic account of the state of society in the town.

Spirituous liquors were freely sold in all the shops, and the inhabitants spent a great part of their time in imbibing them and in playing practical jokes on each other. The hard-drinking blacksmith we had seen drenched was the subject of many of these tipsy pranks. The next morning after our arrival we were told that during the night a party of roysterers had gone to his house, after he had retired, opened a window near the head of his bed, and pulled him out of it, through the window into the open air. This was regarded as a great joke.

On our departure next morning we stopped at one of the shops to make a purchase. The loafers were already at their posts. One of them, as we were about to drive away, remarked, —

"Tell your folks, when you get home, that we are all well here in Bankville, with plenty to eat and drink."

"Especially to drink," replied Jim.

With this parting shot we drove away from Bankville. To do the place justice I must say that on visiting it many years after, when the Maine law had been some time in operation, I saw a marked change in the village. The old, unpainted houses, with hats protruding from the broken windows, had been painted and repaired. Many tasteful dwelling-houses had been built on the main street; the shops were smarter, but had no crowd of drunken idlers around them. The town had become sober, industrious, and prosperous.

In the course of the forenoon we struck the valley of the Saco, in Conway, and the hills began to close around us. We took our noontide meal in a small grove by the roadside, through which ran a babbling brook. While seated here a man came driving down the road in a gig, apparently in some excitement. Seeing us he pulled up and said, —

" Boys, if you are going up the road you may meet a bear. One ran across the road in front of me a few miles back and he frightened my horse so that I have had difficulty in controlling him. I am going down to the village to turn out the hunters."

The man drove on, leaving us much excited by his startling information. The chance of seeing a bear was not to be lost.

"What a pity we did n't bring a gun," said Jim.

We drove on in all haste. Jim was disposed to see a bear in every dog on the road, but bruin had apparently taken to his native haunts, for we saw nothing of him.

Dark clouds had been for some time gathering overhead, and the muttering of distant thunder, with an occasional flash of lightning, gave warning of an approaching shower. The sky momentarily grew blacker and blacker, and seemed to rest like a pall on the top of the high hill under which we were driving. We looked around for shelter, and presently came to a farm-house on the slope of the hill. We drove rapidly down the steep descent into the farm-yard just as the big drops began to fall. The barn doors were wide open, and the farmer, standing in his door, told us to drive in.

On entering the house we found ourselves in a large, low-roofed room. A wide fireplace occupied one side of it. In one corner stood a spinning-wheel, in the other a chest of drawers. From the rafters overhead hung traces of corn and a leg of bacon. An elderly woman sat by the window knitting.

The rain was now descending in torrents, while the thunder reverberated among the hills. We congratulated ourselves on having found so ready a shelter, and remarking on the violence of the storm, the farmer said, —

"Thunder-storms are powerful heavy here in the mountings. This ain't no tech to what we hev sometimes. The biggest storm that ever I knowed," he continued, after a pause, during which a tremendous clap of thunder had shaken the house to its foundation, "was the one that happened nigh on fifteen years ago, when the mounting slid down up in the Notch and buried the Willey family."

"Oh, please tell us about that," said I.

"Wall, ye see, I'd been up to Lancaster, and kim back down through the Notch on'y the day afore it happened. There'd ben a slide, about two months afore that, and it frightened Mr. Willey so much that he thought o' leaving, but he kinder got over it, and thought maybe it would n't happen again. He was living alone up there in the Notch, keeping a kind of a tavern for people that went through. The day I drove down he had just finished repairin' his barn where the slide hit it. I stopped and hed a little talk with him about it, and then drove on.

"A storm hed been a gatherin' for a day or two, and next day it kim on tremendous, I tell you. I never seen no setch down-pour afore or sence. It seemed as if the winders of heaven was all wide open, and the hills was a tumblin' about our ears. I did n't live near the river, but them that come from the Intervale told me they never see the water so high afore. It swept everything clean away.

"Next day a neighbor o' mine kim in, and says he, 'They say the mounting has slid down up in the Notch, and buried up the Willey family.' 'Don't you believe it,' says I. 'I was there on'y day afore yisterday, and they was all right.' Ye see I thought they was talkin' about the fust slide that happened weeks afore.

"But along in the arternoon who should come in but Joe Barker, a man I used to know, an' he said he'd come down through the Notch, an' there'd been another great slide, an' the house was there all ' right, but there was n't nobody in it, an' all the men round in Conway and Bartlett was agoing up to see what had come on 'em.

"I axed Barker how it looked. He said ye never see nuthin'. like it. He was coming down through the Notch afoot, and cal'lated to stop overnight at Willey's. He got there about sundown, and found the haouse desarted. The mounting had slid down back o' the haouse, but had jest gone on both sides of it, and never teched it. There it stood all right, but everything else was buried up.

"Barker, he went into the haouse, an' night coming on he could n't get no furder, so he went to bed all alone in the haouse. He said he hed an awful time of it. He never was so skeered in his life. There was n't no sign of anybody raound, an' yet in the night he kep' ahearing a low moaning saound that made the hair stand right up on his head. It was pitch dark, an' he could n't strike no light ter see where it kim from. It seemed like some poor creetur in distress. He did n't sleep none that night, an' with the first peep o' day he was aout, looking raound. He see the barn was half buried, an' the moanin' kim from one of Mr. Willey's oxen that was crushed under the fallen timbers. He got the critter out, and kim daown to Bartlett an' brought the news to Mr. Willey's father.

·"Wall, next day all the people turned aout, an' went up the Notch. I went along, an' I never see nuthin' like it. You've no idee of the damage the water had done. There was the Intervale all covered with sand and driftwood. The bridges and the fences was all swept away. There was n't no road left. It was all washed aout or kivered over with fallen trees. We had to cross the river in boats, an' on fallen tree-trunks. It was hard gittin' along, I tell ye.

"Wall, when we got to Abel Crawford's haouse, Mrs. Crawford she said she never see no sech flood. The river kim down at a fearful rate, carryin' along sheep an' cattle, an' hay an' grain. Afore she could get her children up-stairs the water was two feet deep on the lower floor. It had put aout her fire and washed the ashes abaout the room. Then the logs kim thumping down agin the haouse till she thought they 'd carry it away. An' there that woman stood all night with her clothes-pole and pushed the logs and timber away as they kim daown agin the haouse. The road was overflowed ten feet deep.

" When we got to the Willey Haouse it was a sorry lookin' sight, I tell ye. You hain't no idee on 't. The mounting had slid, daown back o' the haouse, but a big rock jest behind it had. divided the slide an' it jest went raound the haouse an' never tetched it. Ef they'd on'y stayed in the haouse they'd 'a' ben all right. But of course they was skeered an' run aout o' the haouse, an' the slide jest buried 'em up. There was the Intervale all kivered with rocks and dirt, an' the river choked up, an' nothin' but desolation all raound. The valley was jest kivered with sand and rocks, with a branch of a tree sticking aout of it here an' there. Everything was a heap o' ruins.

" We began a s'arching raound for some o' the fam'ly. I kinder suspicioned that they was buried up in the sand, an' so I looked putty sharp to see ef I could find anything of 'em a stickin' up. through it. I happened to move a twig an' under it I saw some big flies that I knowed was allus raound anything that was dead. I dug daown an' putty soon I saw a hand. We sot to work and got aout the body o' Mrs. Willey. She was dreadfully mangled, but we knowed it was her. Then we found Mr. Willey and his two darters, Eliza Ann an' Sally, an' the two hired men; one of the men, a young feller that I knowed well, had his hand full o' twigs an' branches that he'd caught hold on as the slide swept him along.

"We s'arched a long time, but we never could find the bodies of the other three children. We buried them that we found in one grave, to lay there till we could carry 'em daown to Bartlett, an' Elder Hazeltine he said a solemn prayer over 'em, an' read a passige o' Scripter where it tells about the Almighty who hath measured the waters in the hollow of his hand, and meted aout the heavens with a span, an' comprehended the dust in a measure, an' weighed the mountings in scales an' the hills in a balance, an' the echoes from the mountings repeated every word on 't as plain an' solemn-like as ever ye heerd. I never forgot them words."

"Shall we see the slide on our way up?" asked Jim, after we had sat in silence for a time.

"Sartin, you'll drive right past the Willey Haouse."

The rain continuing to fall, the farmer told us we had better stop all night, and we gladly accepted the invitation. When we asked how much we had to pay, in the morning, our host said he thought he ought to charge us much as twenty-five cents apiece. We thought this very cheap, and speaking of it to an old gentleman whom we afterwards met at Thomas Crawford's, he said it reminded him of an incident which befell him in his youth, while making a pedestrian tour through the Franconia Notch. The party stopped over night at a little hut in the wilds, far from any other house, where an old lady gave them a very hospitable welcome; and set before them for supper a bowl of bread and milk and some wild strawberries. In the morning the same fare served for breakfast. On asking for the bill the old lady said that when anybody came and had supper and stopped all night, and had breakfast, she usually charged six and a quarter cents, but as they had something extra in the way of berries, she thought she ought to charge them as much as eight cents apiece.

Driving on the next morning, the valley grew narrower, and the mountains rose higher on either hand. The Saco, now dwindled to a shallow stream, flowed over its pebbly bed by the side of the road which frequently crossed it.

Presently we came to a gateway, and a man came out of a house at hand and demanded toll.

" Toll," said Jim, " what for?"

"This is a turnpike, and you must pay toll for passing over it."

" How much?"

"Twenty-five cents."

"Twenty-five cents!" repeated Jim, in astonish-, ment and disgust; "isn't there any other way by which we can get through?"

"No, there's only one road through the Notch."

"Well," said Jim, as he reluctantly handed out the silver quarter of a dollar, "I never heard of a country where you had to pay for driving over the roads."

A turnpike was a new idea to us, and we looked upon the levying of toll as akin to highway robbery. The road, we were obliged to confess, was an uncommonly good one, considering the rough character of the country, but it did not strike us that it cost something to keep it in repair.

"We had driven but a few miles farther when we came to a scene that caused us to pause in awe and wonder. The narrow valley was enclosed on either hand by a high mountain wall. On one of them was plainly to be seen the pathway of an avalanche which had swept down across the road, leaving a broad, bare track. The débris filled the valley and was destitude of vegetation, bushes and trees being buried beneath it. The Willey slide was before us in all its desolation. We gazed upon it with an interest heightened by the narrative of the old farmer. Here still lay buried the bodies of the lost children, who, on that dreadful night, rushed into the darkness and the storm, only to meet death in the overwhelming avalanche.

The little house still stood by the roadside, with an addition, offering entertainment to travellers

through the Notch.   We entered it and were shown
the rooms as they were left by the family on the
night of the disaster.   The few articles of rude
and simple furniture had a strange pathos about
them.

Being told by the occupant of the house that it
was but four miles farther to Thomas Crawford's, we
decided to drive on.   The miles proved long and
very much up hill.   The road became rougher.   We
scrambled across ledges through which flowed mountain streams, opening up views of beautiful cascades
as they leaped down from the heights above.   The
mountains on either side closed in with precipitous
walls, and one directly ahead seemed to block the
way.   The road grew steeper, and just where it
seemed to stop and the mountains to shut us in, a
narrow pass opened between the impending walls.
This was the gateway of the Notch, scarcely more
than twenty feet wide, one side of it occupied by the
road, while under the opposite wall flowed the trickling stream to which the Saco was here reduced.

We drove slowly through the gateway, gazing up
with wonder at the perpendicular walls of rock on
either hand.   Just inside the gateway, near a huge
black cliff, resembling an elephant's head, stood the
Notch House, kept by Thomas J. Crawford, a son of
old Abel Crawford, the patriarch of the mountains.

Here we found rest and refreshment, very grateful after the day's adventures.

At eight o'clock next morning the horses were brought to the door. The landlord announced their arrival, and having seen that all things were in readiness, we mounted, preparatory to climbing to the top of the highest peak of the White Mountains. Presently an individual in his shirt-sleeves, wearing a broad felt hat and carrying a staff in his hand, presented himself as the guide.

First came the ascent of the wooded slopes of Mt. Clinton. The path was anything but a smooth one. At first we threaded our way through a deep rut in the earth, anon we were climbing over rocks and brambles, and again we found ourselves ascending a wooden road, which very much resembled a flight of stairs. Turning to the guide for some relief from the tedium of the way, that sapient individual answered all inquiries by saying, "Wall, sir, not knowing I could n't say." He was on foot, and as he occasionally took a short cut across lots, we were at times startled by hearing his voice immediately above us. Presently we came to a spring of water in the woods, where we stopped to quench our thirst and fill our bottles.

Emerging from the woods upon the summit of Mt. Clinton, we caught a glimpse of the sublime

16

scenery which was to reward all our labors. Immediately before us, but with a valley between, Mt.
Pleasant reared its bald head, while behind it rose
Mts. Franklin and Monroe, and towering above all,
like its immortal namesake, was visible the misty
summit of Mt. Washington. The morning clouds
enveloped his head, as though the old gentleman had
not yet pulled off his nightcap.

Crossing the bare, rocky slope of Mt. Clinton,
we began the ascent of Mt. Pleasant. At this
moment a tearing gale swept through the valley,
while the clouds descended from their heights and
completely enveloped us. It was with difficulty we
could keep our seats in our saddles, and the way
seemed lost. But in a few moments the clouds
lifted, the wind swept by, and when we stopped to
take breath upon the summit of Mt. Pleasant, a
magnificent view opened before us. Upon either
hand, far as the eye could reach, appeared innumer-
able hills and mountain, interspersed with beautiful
lakes whose silver surfaces shone brightly in the rays
of the sun, adding a fairy brilliancy to the scene.
Nearer to us, and immediately below, were hills upon
whose sides were the paths of many a land-slide,
while directly before us, and towering far above
Mt. Monroe, stood boldly forth the proud form of
Mt. Washington. Above all, and enclosing all,

towered stupendous piles of white shadowy clouds, like mountains of the air.. As the rays of the sun for a few moments lighted up the scene, it is impossible to conceive anything more beautiful than was the view above and below.

But the guide cried " Forward," and we began the ascent of Mt. Franklin. Here the roughness of the path obliged us to dismount and tread our devious way. Winding around the top of Mt. Monroe, we struck off to the right, and passing under an overhanging cliff, some hundreds of feet in height, where the path ran along the edge of a precipice, nearly two thousand feet high, we found ourselves at the base of the peak of Mt. Washington. Here we paused to take a view of the frightful gorge along whose edge we had just passed. Proceeding onward again, and mounting a small knoll, we were greeted by a beautiful sight. Immediately below us, and enclosed in a sloping hollow, while on every hand arose the rocky summits of the mountains, lay a beautiful lake, — the Lake of the Clouds, — like a lovely maiden sleeping in the arms of a giant. Its tranquil surface as it glistened in the sunlight, contrasting with the rugged peaks around, made our hearts leap, and we shouted with joy on beholding it.

From this point the scenery assumed more and more the aspect of grandeur. We were now ascend-

ing Mount Washington ; on every side nothing
could be seen but the misty outlines of lofty mountains ; before us were the sweeping slopes of the
giant Washington, whose head was enshrouded by
dark, heavy clouds, which looked gloomily down
upon us. Every trace of vegetation had disappeared,
and the mountain seemed an immense mass of
broken rocks, heaped in every conceivable form, pile
upon pile. Above, as far as the eye could pierce the
overhanging gloom, nothing was visible but the same
dark, dull, universal rocks. The mountains whose
summits we had lately thought so lofty were now
sunk into insignificance beneath us. We seemed
isolated from the world, cut off from communion
with mankind, and elevated in solitary grandeur
above their sorrows and their joys.

"Harry," said Jim, "this is almost as terrible as
that night on the ice."

"But fortunately not so dangerous," was my reply.

The clouds came nearer and nearer, and darker
and more sublime grew the scene. It became dangerous to proceed farther with horses, and we therefore dismounted and left them behind. We now
toiled up the steep ascent, completely enveloped in
the clouds, which shut out all view of the surrounding scenery. At length we reached the summit, and
paused for a moment near a monument of stones, to

catch, if possible, a glimpse around.   But the clouds were above, around, below, and we were fain to turn from the works of nature to the wants of man.

The guide produced a pair of saddle-bags, and retiring to a hollow among the rocks, long used for this purpose, we partook of lunch.   While thus engaged the clouds began to break in one direction, and as they slowly rolled aside we caught a distant view, the most sublime we had ever witnessed.   The summits of far-away mountains loomed up in sight, and moving rapidly over them were masses of dark clouds.   While yet gazing on the scene the clouds closed in again, the curtain fell, and we were in darkness again.   Once more they separated sufficiently to disclose to us immense clouds floating past on a level with our position, whose jagged outlines and craggy tops gave them the appearance of moving mountains.   But even as we caught a hasty glimpse of the glories beyond, the same thick curtain fell and all was lost again.

The guide now told us we had remained as long as it was prudent to do so, and descending to the point where we had left our horses we started them before us and trudged on behind.   Presently we met a party of two ladies and gentlemen.   They inquired about the prospect on the summit, but notwithstanding our assurance that little could be seen and the

threatening aspect of the clouds, the ladies, especially the younger one, were determined to proceed,
and when we last saw them they were disappearing
in the all-enveloping clouds.'

It now became safe to mount, and indeed in passing over Mt. Franklin we indulged in a trotting
match, during which I came near tumbling from my
horse with laughter at the doleful grimaces of my
companions, as they bounced up and down. Jim's
horse lagged behind, and we heard in the distance
his perpetual " Get up," as he strove to incite the
lazy beast to a brisker gait. On the summit of
Mt. Clinton we paused to take a last view of Mt.
Washington, and saw that the clouds had nearly disappeared, so that probably the ascending party had
an extended view; yet, as the guide said, " Not knowing, we could n't say."

Plunging into the woods we accomplished the remaining two miles and a half as speedily as possible,
and arrived at Crawford's as the clock struck six.

Determining to proceed on our return home that
night, we set off after supper. Issuing from the gateway of the Notch, Mt. Willard seemed to shut the
gate behind us. The shades of evening were falling in
the narrow pass, and we were impressed by the stupendous mountain walls that shut us in, Mt. Webster rising directly above us and Mt. Willey on the opposite

side. The impending cliffs, in the increasing gloom, seemed ready to launch down upon us. While my thoughts were occupied with the fate of the Willey family, Jim suddenly startled me by remarking, —

"Harry, I don't mean to pay toll on the road again."

"How will you avoid it?"

"I 'll run the toll."

But when we arrived at the toll-house the gate was shut. A woman came out and demanded the toll. After some haggling over a written pass given us by Crawford certifying that we had not passed over the whole length of the turnpike, and were therefore entitled to return for half toll, Jim with much grumbling gave the woman the required fee, and we drove on.

Arriving at the hotel in Conway late in the evening we found it all a light, with much bustle and many teams in the stable yard. Fatigued with the day's climb and the travel of the night, we jumped from the wagon with the loudly expressed determination to go no farther that night. What then was our consternation on being told by the landlord that his house was full, and he could not accommodate us. What were we to do? The landlord said there was a farm-house some miles down the road where we might get accommodation for the night.

Compelled to drive on in the starlit night, we arrived at the farm-house about midnight. The family had long since retired, and all was dark about the premises. After much rapping a gruff voice asked what was wanted.

" Lodging for the night."

" You are late on the road," said the farmer as he let us in.

We were shown to a bedroom back of the living room, on the ground floor, which the farmer and his wife had apparently just vacated.

Exceedingly wearied by the adventures of the day and night, we fell into an uneasy slumber, tossing about until we were completely entangled in the bed clothes. I dreamed that I was climbing the mountain and in the path found a pair of woman's shoes. On awakening in the morning there hung the identical pair of shoes on the wall close at the foot of the bed. In my tossing about in the night I had probably reached up the wall and taken hold of the shoes, which had thus entered into my dream.

The next day's drive carried us back to my aunt's in Bankville. As we neared the village we met nearly the whole population walking and driving towards a common destination. Old farmers and their wives jogged soberly along in their wagons. Young women, on foot, were dressed in their best

The young men carried their Sunday coats under their arms. We wondered what the occasion was that had brought them all out, and on inquiry learned that it was a funeral. Rum-drinking and funerals were the only amusements of these people. The former made them hilarious for a time; the latter afforded a sure opportunity of getting together for social intercourse. At my aunt's we heard more of the riotous pranks of the tipsy Bankvillians, and the wonder grew that any of them were sober enough to attend a funeral.

A long day's drive on the morrow brought us to Landsport at midnight, and we drove through the silent streets as the maidens were bidding their lovers adieu at the doors.

CHAPTER XV.

IN AFTER YEARS.

BOYHOOD is but a dream. How soon we wake up to the realities of life ! Looking back now through the misty years, how rapidly passed those happy days that seemed then so long ; how soon we were called upon to play our parts in the great world that seemed then so far away !

The boys of thirty-five never all met again. After our return from the White Hills, Jim Norton and I soon drifted apart. He took to the sea ; I went to the studies which were to open to me the doors of a profession. Years passed, and only a chance meeting brought any of us together. Gradually we faded from each other's lives, but the recollection of boyhood companionship grew brighter as the years wore on. Now and again a word came, a voice was heard, a strangely altered form was seen for a moment, and then we parted with a pressure of the hand, as ships at sea exchange signals and sail on.

It was many a long year after the events recorded in the earlier chapter of this truthful history that I found myself travelling through the mining regions of California. We had been dragging over the rough road from an early hour in the morning, when we reached a shanty town among the mines, where the stage-coach stopped for dinner.

When I entered the tavern a group of gold-diggers were gathered about the bar listening to the quaint remarks of one of their number. This individual wore a slouch hat, from beneath which fell a tangled shock of fiery red hair. His face was gnarled and his beard was turning gray. He wore the customary red shirt and long-legged boots of the gold-digger, and had even more than the customary swagger. Something about him seemed strangely familiar to me, and yet at the moment I could not place him.

At the dinner-table he took a seat opposite mine. At some remark of a companion he made a grotesque grimace, and then I knew him.

" Neighbor," said I, "you will excuse me, but I would like to ask if you were ever in the city of Landsport ?"

"Landsport !" cried he, half rising from his chair, "I never was anywhere else."

" And do you remember one Harry Ingersoll ?"

He looked at me curiously for a moment, then

jumping from his seat and reaching across the table he grasped me by the hand, and exclaimed, —

"Harry, old pard, this is striking it rich, this is."

We stood a moment with the recollections of other days rolling over us. I answered Tim's eager questions about myself, and then I asked, —

"How long have you been a gold-seeker, Tim?"

"It's too long to remember," said he, a shadow falling over his rugged countenance.

"I hope you have made your pile."

"Nary pile! There's no such luck for Tim Bunce. Though once I struck it rich, but it all slipped away from me."

"Shall we not see you back in Landsport some day?"

He shook his head, and abruptly asked, —

"What has become of all the old boys? Where is Ben Hunter?"

"The last word I had of Ben was in a newspaper account of a great battle of the Rebellion in which it was stated that Col. Ben Hunter was severely wounded while gallantly leading his regiment in a charge upon the enemy."

"Yes," said Tim, "I'll warrant ye he was there and gave the rebs fits," adding, with a humorous grimace, "but he couldn't make a chowder! But do you ever hear anything of Joe?"

"Joe went South and disappeared in the great overturning of the Rebellion. I have never heard of him since."

"And what has become of your crony, Jim Norton?"

"Jim married Susie Stirling, and now commands a fine ship out of Landsport."

"He always took to salt water. Bill Truman went to sea, too, but I suppose he's not captain of a ship yet."

"No, Bill drifted into the navy. When the rebels stole into Landsport harbor and cut out the revenue cutter, a lot of us went on board the steamer 'Chesapeake' in pursuit of them. We had a brass piece on board, and when we neared the cutter a man-o'-war's-man, who had volunteered with the rest, ran to the gun, patted it affectionately, and would have touched it off had not Bill Bigelow interfered and himself applied the match. The sailor was Bill Truman. I had not seen him for years, and I have never seen him since."

"Si Sumner was a home baby, so I suppose he's still living in Landsport."

"No, poor Si died years ago. I was the only one of the boys who attended his funeral."

"And little Ned Thompson, where is he?"

"Ned is running a dry-goods store in Landsport."

"I always thought he was cut out for a counter-jumper."

"The old town is much changed, Tim, since the great fire. You would scarcely know it."

"Then I'll never go back."

"Liberty Street is less changed than many other parts of the town, but our old play-ground in the lumber-yard is gone."

"Is the old stage stable there yet?"

"No, it was long since swept away, and its site is occupied by a block of stores."

"What is Liberty Street without the old stable? No, I'll never go back. But is nothing left of the old town?"

"Yes, the observatory still stands on the hill and displays its flags as of yore."

"I'd go back just to see that, and Diamond Cove."

His voice wavered a little, and I thought I saw a tear gathering in his eye, but it disappeared in one of the customary twitches of his countenance.

Just then the coach was announced, and with many words of farewell and a firm grip of hands we bade each other adieu. As the coach turned the corner of the street I looked back and saw Tim waving his hat in front of the tavern.

I have not seen him since, but as I read in a

California newspaper, the other day, that Timothy Bunce, Esq., was a large stockholder in the Bonanza Mine, I suspect he has "struck it rich," and I should not be surprised any day to see him walk into my office and take me by the hand in his old, hearty way.

www.ingramcontent.com/pod-product-compliance
Lightning Source LLC
Chambersburg PA
CBHW030809020726
47499CB00006B/1832